MW00834882

KAIJU WORLD

R.F. BLACKSTONE

SEVERED PRESS
HOBART TASMANIA

KAIJU WORLD

Copyright © 2019 R.F. Blackstone

WWW.SEVEREDPRESS.COM

All rights reserved. No part of this book may be reproduced or transmitted in any form or by any electronic or mechanical means, including photocopying, recording or by any information and retrieval system, without the written permission of the publisher and author, except where permitted by law. This novel is a work of fiction. Names, characters, places and incidents are the product of the author's imagination, or are used fictitiously. Any resemblance to actual events, locales or persons, living or dead, is purely coincidental.

ISBN: 978-1-925840-47-6

All rights reserved.

This is for Mapi, still believing in me and pushing me to be better and better and for GDT for showing us all that Kaijus can be beautiful amazing monsters.

CHAPTER ONE

Bahía de Acapulco looks simply gorgeous from the beach in front of the Hotel Emporio. The Pacific Ocean is never so inviting or calm, unlike other beaches and coves, most in Mexico are almost perfect. The waves are almost non-existent, just occasional bumps. It's one of the reasons that Acapulco is so popular with tourists. No matter the season, the beaches of Acapulco are always busy.

And today is no exception.

Paragliders sail overhead as children run into and then back out of the cool refreshing water, parents sit in the shade of cabanas, sipping cervezas and tropical cocktails while others sunbathe or frolic in the water. Most ignore the large rock formation called Farallón Del Obispo that sits 200meters in front of Playa Condesa.

It has been there since before anyone can remember. The paragliders can see it clearly and there are many rumours and legends about what it once was and could be.

Only one interests Dutch.

He stands on the ocean's edge and uses high-powered binoculars to look out at the cove. The water laps at his ankles and he sinks into the wet sand, wriggling his large toes to get free.

"Looking good Dutch," a light voice whispers into his ear.

Dutch smiles and wiggles the earpiece. "Don't get used to it, next time you dress skimpily."

The voice laughs, "Are you being a sexist pig?"

"Always Roxie," he retorts, as his free hand pulls the board short wedgie out of his ass. "Any sign?"

"Don't change the subject cum-bucket," Roxie's voice sounds

agitated which gets a large grin from Dutch.

"Too late," he says quickly cutting her off. "Any signs?" Through the earpiece he can hear faint mutterings. *Oh good*, he thinks, *technical problems.* "C'mon!" he says. Quickly he checks his waterproof watch, "The window is closing!"

"We know!" a lilting voice barks back. That's Lawrence, the team's resident tech-monkey. "Johann got the sonar wet."

"You take that back!" Johann's deep accented voice distorts the sound.

Dutch shakes his head. It's rare for him to grow tired of the constant bickering but this is one of the few exceptions. "Children," he says softly enough so that nobody will think he's crazy. "Focus. Do we have a sighting?"

Roxie speaks first, "Nothing yet boss. Sorry."

"Yeah," Lawrence chimes in. "Can't win them all, right?"

Right, Dutch thinks as he stares out at the water. He can feel it. The burn. Already his skin is sizzling and causally he wipes sweat from his face. *Doesn't matter,* he muses sullenly. That's the problem though, it does. It always matters because that is the job and whether they like it or not the team has to deliver. Which is easier said than done. It's been almost a month since they got the order and shipped out to Acapulco, and now all of them have to admit that by the second week they were tired and bored. This is their first hunt in Mexico and Dutch never wants to experience it again. There is only so much sun, sand and cool oceanic waters he can take.

Obviously there have been some perks; like seeing the ocean from a different continent or having proper tacos and not sushi. Dutch hates raw fish...well any fish really, which makes him laugh, considering his job...

The job; standard bag 'em and tag 'em operation but no two jobs have ever been the same since he was hired, *Fuck! Bamboozled is more like it*, he thinks. Since then, he and his team have travelled all over the world at least twenty times and so far, only eight subjects have been caught.

He sighs and thinks about the snows of Alaska. That's where he longs to be, back in the freezing cold. Not the fucking scorching sun. "Fuck the heat," he mutters.

"Amen!" Roxie replies.

"Fuck Gideon Pryke!"

Johann picks up the chorus, "Hallelujah!"

Dutch smiles broadly as he finishes, "And fuck the money!"

"Whoa, there," Lawrence's calm voice takes over the channel. "Now there is something to be said about the evils of capitalism and how it is used to corrupt a man's soul--"

"--Women have rights too!" Roxie butts in.

"Sexist," Lawrence says which is then quickly followed by a loud slap. "Why you have to go and punch me every time?"

"Only until you learn the lesson," her voice is steely.

As Lawrence continues one of his philosophical sermons that none of them cares about except for Lawrence and Johann who uses it as an excuse to make fun of the tech-monkey, Dutch takes a moment and looks out at the ocean. *If I wasn't working,* he ponders, *this might actually be fun.* That's the problem with the job, no free time. Even when they get to sleep they cannot relax properly since any detection needs to be investigated immediately. *Maybe I could retire here,* Dutch wonders as his eyes focus on the shipping container tanker anchored out in the ocean. The binoculars show the name as being the S.S. Venture and he guesses that it is waiting for the signal to come into dock but the man isn't sure how long it's been there for. He lowers them and his eyes linger on a buxom Latina frolicking in the waves.

"Boss," Johann's voice cuts the reverie short. "What's going on?"

The binoculars snap up to his face and Dutch begins scanning the area again, forcing his eyes to find the disturbance.

Nothing!

Lowering the binoculars, he swears to himself. A few children giggle at the new words they've learned. Dutch glares at them which makes them run away, feet kicking up the rapidly retreating water.

The water...

"Scan the lagoon. Ignore anything beyond the heads."

"Dutch, you got a feeling?" Roxie asks, her voice filled with excitement and anticipation. They all know that when Dutch gets a feeling, they best be ready for action.

"Boss always got a feeling," Lawrence laughs.

"Just get on with it," Dutch says softly as his eyes stare at clear blue-green water. It is being pulled out towards Farallón. *Not low tide,* he muses as he looks for a shadow. Around him he can hear the tourists and locals questioning what is going on. Dutch has the answer but there is no way he'll say it out loud. Sometimes even he can't believe his job.

A loud sucking noise causes the gathered people to scream in fright. The wind is being pulled towards the rock formation, as if a plug has been pulled. Dutch watches with a small smile playing on his lips. His eyes stay on the pile of rocks as it begins to shake and move.

"What the hell?"

"The reports didn't say anything about it being that!"

"Boss, what do we do?"

3

Dutch winces from the loud chatter blasting his ear. "Wait," is all he says. His team have been with him long enough to know better than to question him. Stepping onto the now drying sand, he keeps watching and waiting.

Far too small to be the target, he thinks as his mind calculates what category it is. *Can't be anything larger than a kid,* though he needs to be certain. "Scan and give me the category number."

Farallón moves!

At first it is slow and lumbering, just like an old man in a pool. As it tries to pull itself through the suction formed by the waves, a high pitched whining sound deafens everyone. Beneath the noise is a slightly low rumble that reminds Dutch of a thunderstorm. Slowly it begins to pick up speed and the motion smooths out. The remains of the fountain and stairway crack then collapse, crashing into the thing's wake. As it continues moving, the whining grows calmer and deeper, sounding more like a humpback whale's song.

"Category 2!" Roxie's voice is barely audible above the roaring of the waves and the alien whale's song.

"Lawrence!" Dutch shouts over the cacophony of sound. "Boost audio!"

A sudden blasting of feedback deafens him; his face scrunches up in a momentary reaction of pain, then, "Better?"

"Good. Roxie, what Category?"

"Category 2 boss," she sounds shaken which is odd, since finding her Roxie has been the perfect example of cool under fire. For her to be shaken is not good.

"Relax guys," Dutch says calmly. "We've dealt with Kids before. Remember Mozambique? Piece of cake."

"Dutch!" Roxie screams into his ear. "What happened to the tanker?"

The team leader blinks, trying to figure out what the hell the woman is talking about. "Repeat that, Roxie."

"Told you he wasn't paying attention," Johann smugly giggles.

"The shipping tanker. It's gone."

What? How'd I miss that? The binoculars smack him in the face and he feels a sliver of blood. He'll curse about it later. Peering through the glass he cannot see the tanker anymore, there is absolutely no sign of the large vessel except for splashes and waves from the displacement. "What happened?"

"No idea," Roxie says slowly. "We were so focused on the Kid that we lost track..."

"Motherfucker!" this is bad, really bad. Finally, they get their chance and instead of the big prize it looks like another bronze medal. *Pryke's going to be pissed,* Dutch thinks and he knows that he is right. Gideon Pryke, the man behind these expeditions is not one for disappointments, Dutch remembers the last time they came back empty handed. Nobody got their full wage. It sucked but the billionaire had made his point perfectly. It also reminds him of one of the man's favourite saying, "Go big or go home."

"Boss," Roxie interrupts his thoughts again, that's a bad habit he'll have to deal with later. "The Kid. Look."

The beach is empty, which is good. It means that catching the beastie will be easier. Dutch looks at the moving rock formation and his mouth drops open; the thing is bobbing up and down and the sound is now melodic, like it is singing, calling for something.

Or someone.

"We've got a spike on all of the scales," Lawrence speaks quickly. "The sonar shows a massive disturbance while the radar, radiation meters and the Tsuburaya Scale is measuring...Oh God."

"What?" Dutch needs the answer now. "What does the scale say?"

"At least an 85 on the Tsuburaya and the Serizawa reads it as being a 5."

That stops all the chattering instantly. Dutch isn't sure he heard the man correctly but he is also afraid that the man is correct. Taking a deep breath, he asks, "Say that again Lawrence?"

"Give me a moment--"

"We don't have a moment!" Roxie screams. "Serizawa says it's a Category 5. I repeat we've got a motherfucking cunt of a monster coming through."

"You positive?" Dutch needs to be more than one hundred percent sure of the reading. If it's correct then they'll have the biggest catch ever and Mister Pryke will be the happiest asshole on the face of the planet.

"Tsuburaya checks out, ceiling is at 90. I've never seen a reading like this before Boss. How can it be 90?"

Johann laughs, "Because you dumb sumbitch, it's a Category 5! We're rich bitches!"

"Shut it!" Dutch barks. He needs them to be focused if they're going to catch both. They have a plan; all everyone needs to do is follow it.

A water spout erupts into the sky; it is at least over fifty meters high. Dutch's eyes follow it up and he knows that...*What the fuck is that?* It sounds like the crashing of the waves mixed with cannon fire and lightning cracks. Looking around he can only find one place it could possibly be coming from; below the water spout! Dutch watches the water fall back into the ocean. He smiles at the thought of the hefty bonus coming to them all.

"What about the Kid?"

It takes a moment for Roxie's voice to register. "Huh?" Dutch blinks, "Use it as bait."

"No need," Johann says softly.

The tidal wave fast approaching tells him everything. The Category 5 can hear them. A bulge in the water speeds towards what used to be Farallón. The rock formation bounces happily, creating ripples that could be mistaken for large waves.

"It's literally a kid!" Dutch shouts.

"Fan-fucking-tastic," Roxie cheers. "Now, move ya ass!"

The shadow gets his attention. Slowly Dutch looks up and the smile disappears, replaced by awe and wonder.

It's the shipping tanker, soaring through the air spinning on its Y axis. He can just make out the claw scratches, deep gouges from the gigantic talons and the propellers still trying to grip the water and instead churning up nothing but air.

"What are those?"

Dutch knows what Lawrence is referring to. It's the crew or their bodies. They are whipped out and away, splashing into the water hard. He is more than positive each and every man is already dead. At least he hopes they are.

"Dutch."

The voice pushes him and the large man performs an awkward gait through the sand. He can feel the air rush and engulf him as the shadow of the falling tanker grows larger.

"Dutch!" Roxie screams as the ship slams into the sand. Its bulk crushes the wooden cabanas with the impact shoving the sand up and away, creating a crater.

Seconds later the shipping containers follow, raining down around the cracked oil and petrol leaking ship, hitting the sand and white hotels with the force of small meteors. Concrete, glass and furniture tumble to the sand. Some of the less fortunate tourists follow, scraping against the rough walls leaving trails of blood and bone.

From their stations Lawrence, Roxie and Johann stare in disbelief, they have seen destruction before but not on this level or magnitude. "Let's get to work," the woman orders.

CHAPTER TWO

She's running late again. It's the tenth time this week and Mako knows that Mister Pryke won't accept it for much longer. The problem is not her ability to be punctual. Not at all. What keeps her being constantly late is the layout of the facility. Pryke made it too big and it doesn't help that the man himself always gives her five minutes warning before a meeting.

Thankfully below the touristic areas; hotel, souvenir shops, cafeteria/restaurants and the information kiosk, nearly all of the corridors linking the different areas have maps and are clearly signposted. For Mako it is a blessing.

Rounding the corner, the young Japanese woman slides to a halt. As the soles of her shoes slip and skid, her butt hits the linoleum tiled floor and she feels the bruise already start to form.

"Ah! Miss Ikari!" the large booming voice of her boss, Gideon Pryke, echoes throughout the well-lit corridor. "Bully!" her boss extends a hand and trying not to feel too embarrassed, Mako Ikari takes it.

"Thank you," she mutters while putting herself into a semblance of order. Not even thirty years old yet she is already the top in her field, which always makes her laugh.

"What's so funny?" Pryke asks with that same conspiratorial look he always gets when trying to be in on the joke.

Brushing her multi-coloured hair back behind her ears, Mako says, "Just remembering what you said to get me to sign on."

His eyebrows rise inviting her to continue.

"'It's a brave new world'" she does a pretty decent impression of him though the only thing missing is the level of enthusiasm. "'And that means brave leaders.'"

"It's true!" he says beaming at her. His pale eyes twinkle and Pryke expertly loops his arm through hers. "Shall we my dear?"

Mako doesn't speak as the two begin towards the staff canteen. The food and menu are okay but cannot compare to the one in the main guest restaurant. She hasn't eaten there yet, but in the coming hour? A feast awaits!

"So," Pryke begins. "How are the lads?"

"They are neither male nor female," Mako answers, automatically going into work mode. "What we can tell is..." she frowns slightly. "What's so funny?"

Pryke is chuckling and holds up his hand, "My dear, it's an expression! I know they are asexual." His chuckle is infectious and Mako can't help but join in. "But, are they ready for our guests?" he asks.

Pulling out a phablet the woman quickly checks reports and various messages from the different department she commands. Pryke shakes his head and gently pushes the device down, "A simple yes or no will do."

"Maybe," Mako says as they enter the staff canteen. It's busy with most of the administration staff having lunch; a mixture of hamburgers, salads, paninis, yoghurts, chicken tenders and various snacks, all free to the staff. They file past the tables and chairs with Pryke nodding politely at the various employees. The staff wears a mixture of business casual and uniforms while Gideon Pryke himself wears a safari inspired outfit; linen pants, white shirt and a brown leather vest. He carries a Panama hat and cuts quite a figure sliding into one of the booths.

"'Maybe?'" he rolls the word around his mouth like a piece of food. "What's wrong with them? Don't tell me it's a serious case of stage fright?"

Mako shakes her head, "Mister Pryke--"

"--Gideon, Mako."

She clears her throat, "Gideon, these aren't performing monkeys or a flea circus. We have no idea what they are or how they will react to being put on show."

Pryke stares at the menu, focused on what to order. "I think the hot dog will do today." He looks at the scientist, "And for you?"

Food is the last thing on Mako's mind; she can't eat, not until after opening day. Until then she'll keep burning the midnight oil.

"Juan! How is Yuri? Getting over her cold I hope," Pryke booms at the waiter who nods politely, clearly intimidated by the man. Pryke ignores it and continues, "Bully! So, I'll take a hot dog and a triple cheese panini for the talented Miss Ikari here." He has and never has had a problem with ordering for the entire table, as the waiter walks away, he casually checks his watch.

"Gideon," Mako speaks up after a few minutes of silence. "What do you expect to achieve with all of this?" She waves her hand at the room.

"Feed my staff," Pryke says earnestly then starts laughing at his own joke. Mako doesn't even crack a smile. "Oh lighten up Mako. You need to have fun, otherwise what's the point?"

"The point," she says slowly, her eyes boring into his. "The point is that these things are more powerful than Russia's entire nuclear armament. That is the point--" her phablet lights up as notifications take over the screen. Pryke looks amused until his own device follows suit.

"There are guests inbound?!" Mako's voice cracks slightly from the added pressure.

Pryke speaks soothingly, "Don't sound so surprised. You knew about this, remember? Three weeks ago..."

"...I thought you were talking about the Gala Opening."

His smile is full of cheek and he barely hides the amusement in his voice, "Well, yes. But...just make sure our boys are ready."

There is something about his tone that gets her attention. Mako is definitely not buying what the older man is selling. Ever since she was a child her bullshit meter has gotten her out of more trouble and scraps than she can count and right now it is pinging on Gideon Pryke. "Spill, Gideon. What's really going on?"

The showman in Pryke takes over as he grandly declares, "Fame! Fortune! The adventure of a lifetime!" His broad smile and overbearing nature isn't enough to distract her. Slowly the smile disappears as he says, "Have you always been this tough?"

Mako nods and her eyes dart to the two devices; both are still flashing and doing the vibration shuffle. *Lunch will have to wait,* she thinks as the food approaches. Her stomach growls the moment the smells reach her nostrils. Even though it's cafeteria food, Pryke made sure to get gourmet chefs.

"Gracias Juan, much obliged," Pryke says as the trays of food are placed on the plastic topped table. The waiter walks away muttering, "I was born in Chicago. Don't know Spanish from my asshole. But you're welcome." The hot dog is big, almost the same size as a foot long from Subway. Pryke takes a massive bite and savours the symphony of flavours as he chews.

The woman looks at her sandwich, then to her boss and finally to the constantly dancing phone. Mako is torn between her work ethic and the screaming beast she calls her gut.

Sensing this turmoil, Pryke speaks after washing the mouthful of food down with a gulp of soda, "Miss Ikari, when was the last time you ate? I mean properly ate." Mako blushes before sipping from her own soda. Waving a hand in the air, trying to get rid of a bad smell, Pryke remarks, "Well, whatever it is, your team can handle it."

He does have a point, she thinks as the lure of food not from a vending machine wins. Gideon Pryke smiles as she devours the toasted gourmet sandwich. A small moan comes from her as the combination of bread, pepper jack, mozzarella and manchego cheese slides down her throat.

"Good?" Pryke asks with a raised eyebrow.

"Kami! Watashi wa honto no tabemono ga dono yo ni ajiwatta no ka wasurete shimatta," Mako exclaims with such joy it makes Pryke laugh.

"English please. My Japanese isn't that good...yet," he says with a chuckle. "But I can guess what you said."

Mako looks embarrassed as she places the remains of the sandwich back on the plate, "Forgive me Sir. I'll get back to work now."

Pryke looks insulted as the woman stands; shoulders slumped and tears welling up in her eyes. He grabs her wrist, "Stuff and nonsense! Sit down Mako. Enjoy your lunch." His voice is soothing and authoritative as he speaks, "I insist."

Slowly, Mako Ikari sits and begins to eat again. Pryke picks from his large basket of fries, popping the smallest ones into his mouth and leaving the larger for later. He feels Mako's eyes on him and meets them, "Go big or go home."

She coughs and sips from the soda again ignoring his catchphrase, *I'll bring it up later.* Her phone has stopped vibrating from the barrage of notifications and messages but her boss' has not. "It's the guests isn't it?"

The older man blinks, "Beg pardon?" It's rare but sometimes his original accent comes out. "Were we having a conversation I was unaware of?" Most of the staff aren't sure where he is from originally but Mako is positive that once upon a time, Gideon Pryke hailed from London.

"Sorry, still thinking about the inbound guests."

Pryke nods then starts on one of the long fries. Mako watches, then speaks, "They're the reason you're here. Whoever these people are, you're spooked...Did I say that right?" She hates having to ask about her English.

"Perfect!" the man paying the bill beams at her. "And to your assumption, remember what happens." He pauses, waiting for her to ask the logical question. Mako looks expectantly at the man and soon Pryke realizes that she has no intentions of playing the game. "When you assume," he says slowly, "you make an ass out of you."

"And me," Mako says finishing the saying. "Isn't it supposed to be 'and me'?"

He shakes his head, "Not with me." His meaning is perfectly clear and there is something about his tone of voice that makes her feel uneasy.

"Even monkeys fall from trees," Mako says after a moments silence as her eyes go to Pryke's phone. The screen is lit up with an unknown number. "You better get that."

His eyes go to the screen and Pryke seems hesitant as he reaches for the device. He takes a second to answer. "Yes...Uh-huh...Really...? Oh...When did that happen...? Okay...Thank you." The phone disappears into his vest pocket and he smooths back his hair.

"Everything okay?"

"Of course!" he says, that moment of hesitancy long gone. "Excuse me please." He stands, "Our guests are arriving sooner than expected." As he starts to the exit, Gideon Pryke answers Mako's unasked question, "Make sure our boys are ready. The future of us all depends on it."

#

"Two weeks left and not even half the systems online," James McTiernan grumbles as his pale eyes glare at the tablet's screen. He knows it isn't the device's fault but the man's frustration needs an outlet.

The magic number that everyone was working towards seems farther and farther away while also growing larger and deadlier. Originally it was another month before the opening, then for some reason that peacock Pryke brought it forward and nobody can figure out why. That annoys McTiernan more than anything else, not being able to know why something happened. He just will have to add it to the long list of things he doesn't know why. Sighing, he rubs the bridge of his nose and pushes the thoughts of abandoning ship away. *Be a fucking professional*, he admonishes himself. Letting the tablet slide to the steel table before him, McTiernan looks at the rest of the Security Team.

Most, if not all, are ex-military or law enforcement. No mall cops here. That was his one condition for Pryke. Gideon Pryke, a man that McTiernan trusts as far as he can throw him. After their first meeting he called in all of the favours he had in the FBI, CIA and the other sections of the Alphabet. This was done with one single goal; learn everything he can about Pryke and how he amassed his fortune. Unfortunately it was the same way as any other rich man. But he seemed to be one of his word, so McTiernan put together his team and now regrets taking the job.

The control room for all of the facility's operations is down the hall and originally Pryke wanted Security housed there too. There was no way McTiernan was going to let that happen and after almost coming to blows they reached an accord; as long as he does his job and keeps everyone safe and sound then the team can operate from wherever and however they like. This explains the state-of-the-art equipment surrounding him and his men. That was another fight between McTiernan and the walking billfold. For some reason Pryke wanted all of the controls, displays and user interfaces to be touch-screens and holograms. *Like something out of a damn movie,* he thought at the time. Luckily the cost was too much even for Pryke who in the end, as with everything to do with McTiernan, gave in and let the ex-Master Sargent win.

McTiernan loves to win, always has and when the opponent is one of the wealthiest men in the world, winning is everything. The Head of Security scans the large control room and a small smile creeps across his face. They had to rebuild the entire floor to accommodate the consoles and multiple screens. By the end they had a smaller version of NASA control, but instead of scientists and experts running the system they have the best from private security. At least, that is what Pryke was told. For McTiernan, he wanted the best of the best and--

"--Sir, facial recog is malfunctioning again."

"What a surprise," McTiernan mutters as he wanders over to Facial Recognition. It is just one of the many systems that isn't fully operational yet. "What seems to be the problem now?"

Simpson begins to run diagnostics and ignores the imposing presence towering over him. Even though every man on the team would lay down their lives for him, it doesn't mean that they all are intimidated by him. That is the problem with being a Master Sargent in Special Forces.

"Well?" he asks impatiently while placing a hand on the headrest of the ergonomically designed seat.

"The diagnostics seem to take longer and longer each time we run them, Sir."

McTiernan growls, if one system is failing still then that means others will too. He walks away saying, "Do your best." He doesn't want to deal with the dweebs in Programming, but if they want to be fully armed and operational by D-Day, then he'd have to speak with them at some point. He stands erect and clears his throat. Instantly the room goes quiet as the men and women turn, giving him their full attention. McTiernan doesn't bother with pleasantries, he never has cared for them and the team doesn't want them. "How many systems are not functioning correctly?"

John McTiernan does not like to be kept waiting, "How many?" The growl in his voice demands an immediate response.

"The cameras in each enclosure keep giving us misreadings about the assets' locations."

"Which ones?"

"Umm...Infrared, thermal, night vision, standard security...I'm sorry Sir. It's pretty much all of them."

"ID Scanners in the lower levels have problems reading the newest badges assigned."

So far everything sounds like the normal problems. "What about the drones?" That was something he demanded. There are fifteen drones that are constantly in rotation and keeping an eye on all of the enclosures. They call this system of flying cameras God's Eye.

"Fine. The Eye is blinking and doing its job perfectly."

"Excellent," McTiernan is actually relieved.

"We've been experiencing power surges in sectors 3, 8 and 10. It isn't anything major but the Category 3 has been testing the fences."

That's just fucking perfect, McTiernan thinks as the sinking feeling in his stomach deepens. He definitely needs to speak with Programming. Shit. "Is that all?"

"Well, the connection to the weather satellite is gone."

McTiernan laughs; a harsh bark that is completely devoid of humour and emotion. He doesn't say a word as he walks to the door to his private office. As the automatic door silently slides open, he orders, "Somebody get S&P on the line. Get their asses in gear and fix my park!"

Simpson speaks up, "Sir, what will you do?"

The ex-Master Sargent sighs as he steps across the threshold, "Try to figure out how fucked we are."

Inside the office and the moment the door slides shut, the electronic lock clicks and McTiernan slumps into the seat. Unlike most team leaders at the facility, he opted for the same ergonomically styled seat that his team uses. In actual fact his office is spartan; steel table, single screen monitor, mouse and keyboard and nothing else. He doesn't need anything else, for him pictures, posters, any decorations are useless and just become a distraction. Twenty years in the armed forces taught him that. Every single one of his COs had the bare minimum in their offices, whether on the field or at base camp. The lesson stuck with McTiernan.

His phone vibrates and it's Simpson again. Newly recruited and still learning how life is outside of the military, but the thing that does annoy McTiernan the most about him is just how eager he is to make a good impression. "Yeah?"

"S&P are already working on the problems. They believe everything will be up and running before the guests arrive in three hours."

"Good work...wait," McTiernan isn't sure that he heard the man correctly. Even though they have their own communications tower in place, being on an island does make cell phone reception problematic. "What was that about the guests?"

There is a brief pause on the other end and McTiernan can see that the young man is trying to find the right words. "Spit it out."

"A memo was sent to all cells informing us that there is going to be a private tour of the facility starting this afternoon."

Quickly, he checks the notifications on his phone and sure enough there it is, a message directly from the man himself. *That's what you get for leaving it on silent,* he scolds himself. It seems that the older he gets, the less inclined to use modern technology, like the company cell, he is. "Dad, you'd be proud," he whispers as his attention goes back to the young ex-soldier anxiously waiting for the next order. "Good work Simpson. Now have S&P get the facial scanners working yesterday. I want to make sure these 'guests' are the real deal and not Drummond's men."

"Already on your desk," Simpson doesn't miss a beat. "Mister Pryke was kind enough to send us names so that we can put together full dossiers." After such outstanding initiative most TLs would give praise, at least that's what the young man is expecting.

The reality is completely different.

"Listen to me closely Homer," McTiernan uses the boy's nickname. "He may pay the bills, his name is on the stationery and he has more money than God herself."

"Herself?"

"But! That doesn't mean you do anything for him. I am your CO and he is nothing. You get me?!"

The training kicks in and McTiernan watches the young man leap to his feet and shout, "I get you Sir!"

McTiernan hangs up the phone and as the others in the control room begin the hazing, he slumps into the seat and stares at the manila folder. He misses that. The camaraderie that comes from being shot at. Being TL or the CO puts a distance between them and the closeness disappears. All that is left is respect.

A sigh pushes the thoughts away and he focuses on the task at hand: discovering who is so important. The light cardboard silently falls open as he sees five pieces of paper. Each one has an ID photo and basic information. McTiernan doesn't even bother reading the entire dossier, his eyes look for one thing: job title.

It doesn't take him long to find it on each page. "Damn bean counters," he says as he grabs the file and exits his office.

"I want a full workup on these guys now," he barks, tossing the file at one of the men. "We've got VIPs coming and I expect this place to be fully operational...If it isn't? Your last tour of duty will look like a cake walk and I guarantee that cleaning out the Cat 4s will be punishment enough."

"Excuse me Sir," one of the drone operators raises a hand. "A.R.T. are inbound. They have a new asset."

"Oh alert the presses," McTiernan is beyond caring. "Another Cat 1 I suppose."

"No Sir. Their itinerary says it is a Category 5."

#

Dutch stares at the gargantuan shipping container that swings back and forth as the heavy industrial strength cables groan from the weight inside the box. Part of him hopes that at least one of the cables snap, causing the steel encased rectangle to dip at one end and have its contents spill out and crash into the jagged sharp rocks far below the crashing waves of the island. The other part admires how humans will always find a way to solve even the most obtuse problems they could ever encounter.

"How big is it?" Roxie's voice makes him flinch slightly. He didn't hear her approach, which is a rare thing to happen. Either he's getting old or too focused on the task at hand but both aren't good. He quickly looks at her and wishes she would let her hair grow out again; the pixie cut doesn't suit her round face. But he'll never mention that, the last time someone had the nerve to do that ended up with their arms broken in five places and a lengthy stay in the hospital.

"Too big for any of our containment units," Dutch looks at the three trucks hooked up one after the other, ready to pull the heavy and oversized load. That's the thing for Dutch; he saw it up close while Roxie, Johann and Lawrence only got glimpses from the equipment and flashes in the spraying water. He has seen some truly horrendous sights in his life; Nigeria, Rwanda, Mozambique, North Korea and Syria. Even the other categories they have captured are frightening and disgusting to look at, but this? The phrase 'abomination to nature' springs to his mind and Dutch shakes his head as he thinks, *Nothing about this has anything to do with nature.*

"That won't be a problem, boss," Johann chuckles as he climbs out of the lead truck's cab. For an Austrian he doesn't look the way most people expect, the biggest thing is his heritage, though he rarely brings it up and expects nobody else to either. His dark skin glistens in the sun as he begins checking that each of the couplings connecting the trucks to each other is securely fastened. "The original briefing said that any Cat 5's are to be put out into the farthest paddock. That is after being checked, tagged and cleared for the performance that is."

"Why the rush for this one, boss?" Roxie asks as her eyes catch glimpses of the cargo about to be transported. Leathery bumps and ridges that are slick with a mucous that oozes down the sides of the monster inside are visible.

He scratches his chin and tries to ignore the uneasy feeling that is racing up his spine. "Why else? Pryke wants the star attraction for the grand opening. Let's move out."

"Dutch," Lawrence's voice echoes over the dock's speakers. "McTiernan wants to speak with you ASAP. He's saying something about security measures for the new recruit and the incoming guests."

"What guests?" Johann asks as he clambers into the lead truck.

"Fuck me," Dutch mutters as he stalks over to the crew quarters. That was one of the better things that Pryke had built onto the island. Whenever a ship docked, he made sure to have a small motel for the crew of those ships. Sure, they would also get free access to the facility but so far every single one of them have stayed close to the water. What Dutch cannot figure out is why Lawrence is always there, playing cards and exchanging dirty stories.

The buildings are called by the crews and the islands staff a 'motel' but in reality it is a collection of military-style barracks that are surrounded by high electrified fences. At first the crews questioned the fences, but after Pryke tripled their pay they stopped asking questions and just accepted the fact they were making deliveries to an eccentric billionaire's island. Inside the perimeter of the motel is also a control tower, which also doubles as a lighthouse when the storms are raging and the real lighthouse needs help.

Dutch climbs the ladder and watches the convoy of trucks towing the container into the island's interior. He opens the door and steps in. Inside, the room is just above being spartan. There is a single control panel with a couple of screens, standard keyboard and a secondary smaller panel that connects to the high-powered LED light on the top of the tower. "What's this about guests?"

Lawrence looks up from his phone's screen and shrugs, using his chin to point to the landline.

"You're a big fucking help," Dutch says as he goes over and picks up the receiver. "This is Dutch, patch me through to McTiernan." He looks at the philosophy major who is giggling at his phone. "What are you doing?"

"Watching YouTube. I love these imbeciles' takes on Nietzsche," Lawrence laughs as he lowers his legs off of the control panel. The gap between his teeth provides a comical little whistle on certain sounds and words which Johann has no problem with making fun of. Luckily being one of Harvard University's top philosophy students provides him with plenty of witty retorts that usually ends the back and forth quickly. "Do you know what annoys me the most about how Nietzsche has been used?"

Dutch shakes his head, trying with all his might not to engage with the man. *Hurry up McTiernan,* he thinks, hoping that the Head of Security will get to the phone soon.

He isn't that lucky.

"What gets my goat...God I love that expression. What gets me is that he is constantly being dragged all over the world, y'know? He goes from being this great intellectual thinker with all of these amazing and brilliant things to say about life and the harshness found within, then he appears in memes and bad motivational posts. Completely misquoted, mind you!"

Dutch holds up his free hand which silences the other man instantly. "McTiernan, the new assest is being transported to the Cage right now."

"Wonderful news!" McTiernan's voice has that sense of false happiness. "Once that's done would you and your team mind heading to your dorms? You've been working oh so hard and need a rest."

Dutch chuckles at the over the top act of civility. Since day one neither man have liked or accepted the other. They know why though; each one came from a different branch of the military. Sure, there is mutual respect but that's all. "That is so kind of you," Dutch answers with almost the same level of civility. "But perhaps you can answer me--"

"--Cut the shit," McTiernan lost the battle. "We've got guests inbound. Investors, which means..."

"Which means everything has got to act like it is the real deal."

"Good man," the voice on the other end of the phone sounds happy but is becoming increasingly distracted. "Is there anything else?"

Dutch sighs, "No. Tell the Big Man we'll keep out of the way."

There is no reply except for the abrupt and tell-tale click of the phone being hung up. Slowly, the large man puts it back into its cradle then stares out at the sea.

After a few seconds of silence, Lawrence speaks, "Should've stayed retired, eh?"

#

The trucks thunder along the newly asphalted road. The oversized tires grip the road tightly, minimizing the swaying of the humongous trailer. Periodically a deep rumbling is emitted which is quickly followed by a smaller growl.

"That's starting to annoy me." Roxie slams her fist into the metal back of the cab. Even over the roar of the three heavy duty engine blocks and the rolling of the tires, the sounds behind them cut over all other noises. She growls as she and Johann bounce and try desperately not to slam into each other.

"You don't say?" Johann smirks as he swerves, trying to miss a small rat scurrying across the road. "I thought it provided a nice refrain from the jungle sounds." His smile says it all before his attention returns to the road.

"A regular Mister Rogers you are."

"Oh yes, just blacker and with a much bigger cock."

Both laugh as the rumbling continues behind them. Apart from Dutch, Johann is the only one Roxie can really be herself around. "Stop being a drongo!"

"What the hell is a drongo? Speak English for fuck sake, or at least close enough, you Convict." Johann winces from the fast punch to his arm. He cries out and goes to rub it then quickly remembers the road, the trucks and the precious cargo. "Bitch."

"You love me," she says with a big grin. Roxie looks out the window and the smile fades slowly. Whenever she sees the trees rushing by and feels the wind in her hair and smells water close by, her mind, for some reason, instinctively goes to her old job. The one she used to have in Australia, which was the reason Dutch and Mister Pryke hired her. Growing up in the Outback of Australia doesn't give a girl many chances in life. So when she found a job in the swamps of the Northern Territory that made some of the best money in the entire country, a young Roxie went to work for the country's largest crocodile leather farms. The job was surprisingly easy but with a certain element of danger; two men teams would go out into the swamps then they would go up in a helicopter and search for a nest. Once they had located it, Roxie would be lowered into the muck and her job was to distract and lure the very big, very strong and very angry mother croc away. While she was being chased, the other would lower himself down and collect the eggs. If the prehistoric monster got to her, then it was game over. If not, her partner would swing round and literally pick her up. It was a fun exciting job that taught her a lot. Four years is how long she lasted until the day she saw a man get mauled by the beast, he had tripped and landed in a pool and as everyone knows crocodiles are faster in water than on land. The poor bastard didn't stand a chance...*Didn't stand a chance,* she thinks.

"Hey! Hey! You listening to me?"

She blinks and turns to see Johann looking her at curiously.

"What?"

"Listen."

It takes a second for her to realize that they have stopped moving. Quickly, Roxie tilts her head and lets the outside world invade her ears; trees rustling in the breeze, birds chirping and the occasional small animal disturbing the undergrowth. She has no idea what to listen for. "What--"

"--Behind us."

Roxie's breath catches as she understands the problem. There is no rumbling from the cargo! What could have happened to make it go quiet? Since getting the job and joining Dutch's team she has seen some truly frightening shit, but absolute silence terrifies her to the bone. "I'll go check."

Johann shakes his head, "Too risky. You stay here and call for backup."

"What about you?"

He shrugs happily, "Maybe this will be my time."

Before she can say anything, the door is open and the man scrambles down, whistling a merry tune. The door swings back and forth slightly when it is caught by the breeze. Roxie doesn't waste any time and grabs the radio, "This is A.R.T. One, come in Cage. Come in."

"Roxie?"

"Dwayne! Is everything ready for our new guest? We're close but Johann thinks there might be a problem."

She waits anxiously as the static screams at her. They have never brought in a Category 5 and none of them want to find out what sort of destruction it can do. The predictions say that it would be worse than every nuke going off at once. "Yeah, Doctor Ikari is waiting for you. Do you need backup?"

"Nah," Johann says after grabbing the radio from Roxie.

The truck roars to life and they continue on. The radio rattles since the man didn't put it back properly. Roughly, Roxie reattaches it then glares out the window. "So..." he says after a moment, "Want to know why it went quiet?"

She shakes her head with a grunt.

"Would you believe," he says anyway, "that it was asleep?"

"Suppose even those things need to sleep at some point."

Johann nods as the guard towers of the Cage come into view. Even though they call it 'The Cage', in reality it is the containment area for everything that the Asset Recruitment Team that Dutch runs bring in. Roxie hates it due to the fact that Doctor Mako Ikari has to run tests on each and every one of the subjects before it can be out into a paddock. "Let me out here. You've got this."

He pretends not to hear her as they pass through the security gate. "Fuck you," she snarls.

"Such language! Do you kiss your mother with that mouth?"

As he manoeuvres the load, carefully backing it into the loading bay, he cries out from the rapid punches that connect with his shoulder. "Sorry," he says realizing the faux pa he just made.

Roxie doesn't answer as she leaps from the cab and stalks away, heading for the walkway that connects the Cage to the rest of the facility. Johann watches the Cage crew hook the container up to a chain line and slowly drag it into the multi-layered subterranean building. As it vanishes into the darkness, a snarling rumbling roar similar to the sound of a building collapsing, surrounds him. In the years that he has done this Johann cannot remember a single time he truly felt afraid. He shakes his head as he mutters, "They ain't paying us enough."

CHAPTER THREE

The two hundred and fifty foot superyacht, the S.S. Cooper, rises and falls with the waves. She has an impressive look, gliding through the sea; the sleek design helps her to cut through the waves at a cruising speed of sixteen knots. Including this and her buoyancy makes the continuous rolling feel gentle.

On deck, that is.

Below in one of the nine luxuriously appointed cabins, the five men all grip the oak table as if their lives depend on it. It doesn't matter that this yacht, built by Icon, has all of the most advanced safety features available to the most financially sound buyer, they are still unimpressed with the situation. Each one silently curses himself for even agreeing to the trip.

"Why didn't we take the cunt helicopter?" Emmerich asks, his German accent showing itself again. Big and burly, the others know better than to get into a fight with him. A fact that has made him think that he is the Alpha, and as such he acts accordingly.

"Because," Crichton says with his usual calm demeanour, "our host said those magic words: 'cost effective'. Hence..."

Emmerich snorts and then looks at his phone. At least the yacht has access to a satellite which provides some of the best internet speeds available on the seas. Each of the other men decides to follow suit, hoping to distract themselves from the buffeting of the waves. "At least he isn't like Drummond. That whole 'spare no expense' spiel, always hated it," Beacham laughs at the memory.

They had been lucky; originally their firm had been approached by the noted industrialist, Sean Drummond. He wanted them to invest in his little theme park but after performing a thorough risk analysis the five partners decided no.

"At least with him," Tull sighs, "we'd be in the Caribbean."

Some of the others nod in agreement. Only Beacham and Emmerich remain quiet.

It was one of the greatest PR disasters in the history of PR problems. Drummond had always been in competition with Pryke and cut corners to get his park open first, the only extreme family theme park. Drummond used the phrase 'the first truly immersive wildlife reserve', when in actual fact it was a zoo for genetic monstrosities. Dino Park opened to great acclaim and high box office, but when a hurricane hit the park and power was lost, the genetically engineered dinosaurs escaped and attacked. Three hundred and fifty guests and employees were killed or seriously injured. And Drummond vanished into the justice system.

Emmerich laughs that bark of his, "Yes and also bankrupt."

"Or worse. Eaten," Beacham adds.

The only one who hasn't spoken yet is Winston. The most senior of them all, his size hides his speed. And like every other aspect of his life, the boulder of a man does not waste his words. "Delvin," he rumbles, his teeth barely parting.

The other four men stare at the giant. After twenty years, one would think they could follow the single word ideas. Winston says nothing as his hands fondle the large heavy crystal whisky glass.

"I'm sure that makes perfect sense," Tull sneers. "But for the rest of us mere mortals, care to elaborate?"

"This should be good," Emmerich mutters.

The smile that creeps across the heavily lined face is unnerving. "You're right. Drummond would've been a good bet. That park of his easily should have brought in at least billions of dollars per year. And that is the problem with you young fucks." He continues talking over the protests, "Because of the internet, all of you are used to instant gratification. Which means that-- Be quiet!"

His roar stuns the four men. They have never heard him raise his voice before. Emmerich and Tull try not to giggle at the sight; Winston's face is a bright crimson, his eyes bulging and at any second now will pop out, as will the veins on his neck, thick and pumping with blood. "Let me remind you," he says trying to calm himself. "That if it had not been for me, all of you right now would be in the exact same place as Devlin. Working at McDonalds. So, show some fucking gratitude."

Winston's eyes scan the room, locking with each of his younger partners. It helps him, every now and then, to re-establish his dominance. Each man looks away except for Crichton. He and Winston have an uneasy alliance, for how long neither man can say.

"So," Crichton begins. "What is the point?"

A deep chuckling fills the luxurious cabin. Winston heaves himself up to his feet and makes his way to the bar. He moves with the motion of the waves easily and as he carefully peruses the selection, he speaks. "It's simple. Return of Investment; how much we put in compared to what we get back. Drummond looked like a sure bet. His books proved that. But he was bullshitting like there was no tomorrow. I can't abide that."

"Okay," Emmerich cuts in. "What makes Gideon Pryke such an angel?"

Crichton is the one to answer, "He isn't. But, he has been open and--"

A gentle tapping on the wooden double doors stops him talking. All eyes go straight to it as one of the handles clicks and the door glides open. A very pretty woman sticks her head in. "Forgive the intrusion," her voice has just the slightest tinge of a Japanese accent. "We have arrived and Mister Gideon Pryke welcomes you."

#

"Don't do anything till I'm there," Mako Ikari orders into the cell phone. Her heels clack loudly on the linoleum floor and the sound grates on her ears. *Always has, always will,* she thinks as she turns a corner and pushes past a pair of low-level techies.

"But Professor, Mister Pryke wants the asset prepped and ready for the guests," the nervous voice on the other end says. It is slightly familiar to her but definitely a new guy. She wants to say it belongs to Preston...Yeah it is Lathrop Preston, Mako is positive of it. "Professor?" Preston's voice brings her back to the here and now.

Mako rolls her eyes and stops. She is in front of a large security door, one of the many that separates the various departments of the facility. This one leads into the labyrinthine corridors that connect Control and the Visitor Centre with Security, Containment, Medical and the living quarters for the staff. Quickly she scans her ID badge, presses her thumb to the bio-reader and then waits. "With all due respect to Mister Pryke," she says, fighting her strict Japanese upbringing to be constantly polite. "But he can 'ask' for anything he wants. That's what being an eccentric billionaire means. So, let me ask you something. Who gave you the job?"

The door hisses as it slides open slowly and Preston says, "You did Professor Ikari."

Mako takes off at a full run and as her feet pound the floor, she fist pumps the air, "Good. So, what will you do now?"

"Follow the protocol set down by you and not worry about Mister Pryke's schedule," even though the techie says the words there is a distinct lack of conviction to the quivering voice.

"Excellent!" Mako says turning a corner and wishing that Pryke had ordered the Segways he originally promised. "You'll be a fine biologist one day."

Preston sighs, "Gee thanks. Ummm how are we going to scan it? We've never had to deal with an 'adult' before."

"No. Don't use those stupid nicknames that A.R.T. gave them. You must treat them with the respect and deference they deserve. We are not going to fall into the same trap as Drummond and Dino Park. So, use their categories, please," Mako's voice is the same as a mother chiding a child. "I'll be there soon."

Before Preston can answer, Mako hangs up and then quickly scans her screen, checking the notifications and hoping that nothing major or more important has come up. There is no way that Mako Ikari would let someone else perform the initial scans, tests and diagnostics on the first Category 5 in the short history of the planet. Luckily there isn't anything that relates to her or her crew.

Mako's eyes scan the signs and markings, making sure that she is heading in the right direction. That's the last thing she needs, to be late and letting the techies do it. *One hundred meters or so*, she thinks as the klaxons close to Containment begin sounding off.

Both of her shoes, practical not fashionable no matter what Gideon Pryke tells her, smack the floor and the echo keeps pushing her. Ever since she was a child, Mako has used the sounds of her feet in an empty space to go faster. She imagines herself being chased by some giant monster with one single intention: to kill and eat her. Luckily, working for Pryke has put her in close proximity to the very same monsters of her nightmares so the imagination isn't that hard to pull from.

She spots the security doors that lead into the personnel scanners that then pass into the decontamination chamber. Mako hates the whole process, having to strip down and be sprayed with a noxious mixture of cleansers and bacterial killers. But, that is the way things have to be done. Once the asset is scanned, probed and given the all clear it will then be given a paddock on the island and set free, able to roam its area and then be transported when needed for the guests.

As she waits for the spray, her mind wanders to the idea of Pryke's endeavour and how, to her at least, the entire idea is one that reminds Mako of the old sideshows and penny gaffs her father told her about. *Why not tell him about your worries?* she thinks. But, the answer is always the same. Gideon Pryke never listens to anyone other than himself, except when it comes to technology or expertise.

"Professor Ikari," the man himself speaks over the intercom. "How much longer until the new recruit is ready for a show?"

Mako slams her fist against the speaker button and talks while trying not to breathe, not an easy task. "I'm just about to begin Gideon."

"That's not what I asked Mako," Pryke's tone is one of slight disapproval.

She sighs and coughs, "Two hours, maybe. Its size is the factor we're not sure about. Could be longer."

There are seconds of static before Pryke answers, "Get it done ASAP...Please."

The decontamination finishes with high-powered fans sucking up the excess mist, the sudden gust of wind blows her hair around and Mako giggles as the door slides open and she walks into her home away from home. Asset Containment.

#

"Should have learned from Uncle Walt," Gideon Pryke mumbles as he stands on the edge of the long wide pier. The island has two docks; the southern one is the smaller of the two and is used for loading and unloading cargo, assets and personnel. The one he stands on is three times the size and has only one purpose, load and unload the guests.

He squints and looks up at the sky, his Panama hat helping to keep the sun out of his eyes. All his life Pryke has wanted to beat his childhood idol, Walt Disney. Both his parents never understood it but were happy with the drive it gave their son in school and then university. "Sir," the dock master, Bob, says trying his best not to disturb his boss. "The ship's almost in."

"Excellent! Thank you Bob," Pryke says before moving closer to the edge of the pier. He glances into the clear inviting water and his mind goes to Disney. The story that gave Pryke the younger the million dollar idea was when Disney opened the original Disneyland. Even now, with all the tension and pressure, it still makes him smile. Nineteen fifty-five and Uncle Walt opened the original park in Anaheim, California. One could say it was a disaster; over twenty-eight thousand people showed up with more than half sneaking in or buying fake tickets. A plumber's strike forced Disney to choose between either working fountains or functioning toilets. The great man chose the facilities. Freshly poured asphalt was still soft and trapped many women's high-heeled shoes all while the entire shindig was being televised.

For Pryke, hearing about one of the world's great entertainers failing so spectacularly, was just the right catalyst. But even with all of his money, the best people and top of the line technology and equipment, there are still things going wrong; whether it's new assets, the asset not being prepped yet or power fluctuations plaguing certain systems. "It never ends."

His private superyacht's horn announces to everyone there that it is time for them to get working. Pryke steps aside and watches as the dock workers ready the heavy-duty ropes, check their phones and generally wait.

Gideon Pryke smiles as the bow of the yacht comes into view, cutting the water easily. He can see the five suited men standing on the starboard side. Each one is in full business attire. Pryke chuckles, *Hope they brought shorts.*

The workers get to work, tossing the ropes to the seamen waiting on deck, guiding the large vessel close enough to the pier. *We'll have to automatize all of this*, he thinks and Sean Drummond's favourite saying pops into his head; Spare no expense. *Yeah right, look where that got you.* His eyes go to the five men and he chuckles as the gangway is lowered and his VIPs begin disembarking. Pryke smiles broadly and extends both arms openly, "Gentlemen! Welcome! Welcome to--"

"--Cut the pleasantries," Emmerich barks. "I need solid fucking ground." He pushes past Crichton who is helping Winston. The older man stumbles from the sudden movement and nearly topples over the side but Tull and Crichton catch him by the arms.

Pryke holds out a hand but the German ignores it, instead he turns and looks back out to sea. In the distance the faint outline of a city can be made out. "Is that Tokyo? Doesn't look that far away," Emmerich says with a snort.

As the other four men step onto the pier, Pryke shakes each of their hands enthusiastically. "No, that's Chiba," he says offhandedly. "Gentlemen!" his voice rings clearly and Emmerich has to turn to listen. "I know that the journey from Tokyo to here was hard. But now, how about a pleasant drive and we'll get you settled?"

Beacham spots the open topped customized Hummer, "I thought we'd go by limo or a train system."

"Where's your spirit of adventure?" Pryke sounds incredulous. "Part of this endeavour is to get people back in touch with Mother Nature. Besides," he pats Beacham's back, "a little time away from civilization is good for the soul." He is all smiles as he climbs easily into the vehicle. Without a word, the group of investors struggle to get in. Winston, even with his girth, is the first to make it in. The others soon follow. "Right!

Let's crack on!"

"So, if we're escaping civilization," Tull says as the Hummer hits a still needing to be paved dirt road. "Then where are we headed?"

As they bounce and try not to slam into each other, Gideon Pryke looks back at them and smiles mischievously, "Where there be monsters."

#

"Wow...that's huge!" Lathrop Preston whispers after a few minutes of stunned silence.

Mako has to agree, though for her she still hasn't recovered the ability to speak. From the moment Johann delivered the container to now, every member of her team has been absolutely gobsmacked. *It must be at least one hundred fifty meters tall,* she thinks.

From inside the container, rumbling can be heard. It sounds almost like purring. Mako glances at the rest of her crew standing around her. All of them have the exact same expression; shock, awe and just a little bit of pee-their-pants fear. The purring breaks Mako's reverie and she snaps her fingers, "Okay ladies and gents." Her voice instantly grabs the attention of her people, "You know the drill. Only difference is size. Let's start with the measurements. General ones."

Without any other sound the control room erupts into a flurry of movement, some are quickly recalibrating the more finicky scanners, others start warming up the cranes and robotic arms. Only Mako remains motionless, her eyes fixated on the large container that is vibrating rapidly.

"Professor?" Preston's voice sounds faint. "Shouldn't we sedate it?"

She stands, saying, "Not until we weigh it." Her hands glide over the control panel until she finds the main crane control. "Once we do that, then we can figure out the correct dosage," Mako stares at the man. "Or do you want to kill it?" That is the thing about her, around most people she is demure but put her with her team and she opens up and has no problems speaking her mind.

Preston says nothing as he goes over to his station and watches the life signs and vitals of the creature. So far they all read normal. Bur for what they are dealing with, normal is an extremely subjective term. He doesn't bother watching his screens; unless something catastrophic occurs then the readings shouldn't change much.

His eyes stare at the giant container. Every eye is on it, and why shouldn't they be? Five years of waiting for a sign, any detection and then the hope that after capture the asset will be suitable. Even after all of the tests, probing and scanning, the final decision always goes to Gideon Pryke. There have been many that he deemed not worthy enough; whether it be the abilities are not eye-catching, not powerful enough or most importantly, completely unappealing to the eye. If he says no for any reason...then Mako gets a dissection partner.

Mako is able to control the cranes easily. Growing up with a father and brothers in construction helped. Her hands glide with the joysticks and they move smoothly, the hooks catching the rings expertly. Her crew are amazed with the skill she has and the fact that they cannot hear a single thing on the other side of the blast proof glass. There are microphones laced throughout the warehouse sized centre which feeds them the purring.

"How heavy is the container?" Mako asks as the heavy-duty chains strain and stretch.

Slowly the container begins to rise, inching off of the ground. Mako can see the cranes bend slightly. "How heavy?" she barks.

Julayne answers quickly, "At least a hundred tonnes."

"Okay," Mako says, feeling a little calmer now. "Is the scale ready?" She doesn't wait for an answer and swings it to the right. The chains groan under the stress.

"Don't drop it yet!"

Mako ignores Julayne as her eyes are focused on the chains. Even though these are similar to the type of chain used at the shipyards, she can tell that each link is close to the breaking point. "No choice."

The container sails down towards the giant digital scale. Mako prays that the steel structure doesn't crack. "Hughes," she addresses Julayne by her last name. "What is the probability that--"

The loud crash shakes the building and instinctively a few of the team dive under their consoles. Even Mako is a little unnerved by it, "Is it cracked?"

Carsten uses the 4k cameras mounted on the underside of drones to perform a quick inspection. "No signs of damage." The image is clearer than real life and the technogeek loves his job.

The collective sigh is followed by a wave of giggles. Not one asset inspection has gone smoothly. It seems to be the tradition and Mako should have been expecting it.

"There it is," Brad Carsten says, wiping a foam moustache from his own bushy magnum.

Mako Ikari is over and bending slightly to see the large twenty-seven inch screens. "Where?"

Carsten doesn't need to point it out as the drone gets closer to the jagged slash of metal. "Good," Mako says. The crack is nowhere near being big enough for the asset to escape through. *Unless it can shrink its physical form,* Mako thinks with a slight shudder.

"Hey, check this out," the video expert says just loud enough for everyone else to hear. They glance at his screens and gasp.

There is a slight glow coming from inside the dark container. It is a deep blue and seems to pulse as the source moves about rapidly. "Is it radioactive?" Preston asks softly.

"What the..." Mako breathes.

The giant eye opens, exposing the brightly shining ocular orb. The blue is coming not from the iris, but the entire organ. The whites are a slightly lighter blue while the veins and scar tissue are darker shades of blue. There is not one area that is not the unholy blue.

Mako looks around in horror. "Lower the blast shields!"

It takes a moment for the lead-lined heavy duty shields to begin their descent and as they do, the rest of her team start to look around and some of them scream in fright and disgust. Their skeletons are visible in the light from the eye and the sight of half and quarter skeletons moving about and wearing clothes is an extremely disturbing thing to behold.

When the shutters finally close, Mako is the only person to speak, "Everyone needs to get checked out by Medical. No excuses and no working until I see the report saying so. There is no way of telling how much radiation we were just exposed to."

As her team begins to calm themselves, Carsten trembles, "Mako, you really need to hear this..." Without warning he turns up the speakers and the most terrifying sound any of them have ever heard fills the control centre.

It is that deep rumble again but this time it is mixed with a coarse, slightly higher pitched scratching. The sounds remind Mako of the old well wheel on her grandparents' land. The entire thing is rhythmic in its pulsing tone. It sounds almost the same as...

"Is it laughing?"

#

The black Hummer bounces roughly as it speeds along the dirt path. Gideon Pryke whoops and he has to clamp a hand down on his Panama hat. To the driver, his boss looks like a cowboy who also happens to act like one. For the five suited men crammed into the back two compartments, the entire act is starting to wear thin.

"Don't you have fucking roads here?" of course Emmerich is the one to share his thoughts.

Pryke says nothing but points at the side of the road where all of the equipment needed to lay asphalt and then pave the road waits. "We've already started, oh don't you worry. It'll all be done before we open."

A sharp turn and they careen down a slope. The investors close their eyes and wait for the inevitable crash.

Instead the large tires smack into a lip of fresh laid road and they hear the low growl of the tires on asphalt. "Ah," Pryke chirps happily. "Now, any questions?"

His cheerful smile infuriates all but Winston and Crichton who are used to the billionaire's personality. Most of the men look to Emmerich again to be their collective voice. He looks at the lush green foliage whipping past them; a sigh escapes his mouth as Emmerich enjoys the breeze.

"What are you doing here?" Beacham speaks up.

Pryke's laugh is loud and a little childish. "Taking you to our five star hotel." He waits for at least one of his investors to crack a smile. When he realizes that won't happen, Gideon Pryke presses on, "Yes. Well, this little weekend getaway is to show you exactly where your money went--"

"--All four point eight billion dollars," Tull exclaims.

Pryke nods, "Exactly. So, firstly allow me to welcome you to Maikeru Island. Two billion dollars went to purchasing the land rights. No way would I rent, the rates would be astronomical." Now that the road is smooth, his audience has visibly relaxed. "Luckily we have plenty of governmental contacts at Chiba, a mere seventy-two odd kilometres from us. The rest of your money and some of my own has gone to setting up this nature reservation," he explains.

"What kind of reservation?" Winston growls.

"Ah, that is the sixty-four million dollar question." Pryke is having the time of his life. "Do you remember the attack on Tokyo from about ten years ago?" He isn't surprised one bit by the blank stares. Most people don't care to remember the tragedy. All of Japan does and every year they have a national day of mourning.

"Something came out of the water and destroyed almost seventy percent of the city," Pryke is now sombre. "A joint effort between nearly all of the Pacific Rim took almost three weeks and millions of lives to bring it down. It took Japan close to five years to rebuild. Our payment for the island helped massively which is also why we have been left alone."

"What was it?" Tull asks with the same tone as that of a child. "What attacked?"

Pryke chuckles as he speaks, "A giant creature that they thought was an undiscovered dinosaur, then there was the idea that it could have been a mutation caused by contaminated water in the bay." He wipes his face. "In English we have no name for what it is. But, the Japanese?"

He lets the question hang in the air as the vehicle crests a small incline and the facility comes into view; every single building is modelled on Japanese architecture. Each one has red tiled roofs and varies in sizes. The men gasp as they see the main gate, it is at least thirty meters tall, the sign written in a distinct font; it looks just like a paintbrush but the edges are too sharp.

"Kaijus," Pryke says. "We're a Kaiju reservation."

The Hummer passes under the gate and each man reads the sign: KAIJU WORLD WELCOMES YOU.

CHAPTER FOUR

The woman stalks down the wooden pier. Her dark eyes dart back and forth, scanning her surroundings for any possible hostiles. Even with her training there is always the possibility of a surprise attack. Ellen Scott stops and stares at a collection of fishermen. Each one holds up an odd looking marine animal and speaks rapidly, then at the end of their story the others laugh loudly.

Fucking Tokyo, she thinks. *No respect for any living creature.* Part of her wants to spit at the men, kick their buckets into the water and watch the catches swim away. Then again, the rest of her does understand that with the reconstruction and slow rebirth of the city and its economy that these men need to find any reason to laugh. Ellen shakes her head and reminds herself about the job and that animals come first, so she continues on, her combat boots pounding on the wood.

Where's the boat? That is one of the more pressing questions plaguing her mind. Even after the tragedy of ten years ago, she expected Tokyo Bay and its harbor to be organized and well maintained. The complete opposite is the case; there are clumps of trash and plastic floating in the water that is mixed with oils and petrol. *How many turtles and fish are going to die?* Ellen's nose wrinkles up as the foul stench of decaying flesh and fish scales bombards her sinuses. *How did it all come to this?*

Her thoughts crash through her mind and just to distract herself, Ellen glances at the screen of her phone, she hasn't closed the message app since receiving the all-clear. There is only the one which reads: TOKYO BAY. PIER 50. BERTH 12A. NOON. So far she has been to five different Pier 50s and naturally Ellen has begun to lose her patience.

One more try, she thinks. Again.

Ellen's eyes dart out to sea and she frowns. The waves are large and ominous looking with the water looking a dark aqua. "Fuck," she says as the tall woman hopes that the boat they've rented will be sturdy enough for the journey.

She continues along the pier ignoring the cat-calls and whistles from the old and young alike. As she keeps searching for the right pier and correct berth, her mind wanders and absently she touches the sewn-on patch that covers her right breast pocket; it looks like something out of 'Animal Farm' only more stylized. A series of animal paws and hooves form a circle, each one touching the other in a show of unity. Below that is a motto in Latin: MORS PRIUS SERVITUTEM and below that is the name of her organization: ANIMAL ALLIANCE.

Since she was a teenager her life has always been about the Alliance. It started since she saved a Golden Retriever from being stomped to death by a group of hooligans. She joined PETA but hated the political machinations of the group, that was when her Aunt introduced her to the Alliance and immediately Ellen joined. Her Aunt was proud as punch, but both of Ellen's parents were furious, so much in fact that they disowned her and severed all contact. The tall blond hasn't had any contact with them for over twenty years. Naturally there have been times when she has wondered how they are or what their lives have been like. Then there is a new job and the thoughts disappear.

"Ellen!" the voice grabs her attention.

She spins her head and she could strangle Lloyd Behm for screaming her name. The new recruit waves enthusiastically at her, trying to show her where the rest of the team is. Her heavy boots thump on the wood and many fishermen have to duck out of the way before being trampled.

Lloyd stops waving and looks at the three other men who are trying not to laugh. "What..." The realization hits him and he too laughs, "Fuck you guys!"

Rick Shaw is the first to stop laughing, his girth swaying with each convulsion of his body. The large smile is easy-going and relaxing, but it is when he speaks that surprises people. A voice that rumbles from deep in the chest, "You're not one of us--"

"--Gooble Gooble! One of us!" the dwarf, Christopher Michael sings gleefully.

Shaw shakes his head and kicks the foot, instantly shutting up the small man. He clears his throat and continues, "Ignore him, his size makes him more annoying than anyone else."

"I hope you get fucked by a fish."

Lloyd blinks. "That's a little unnecessary." He gasps and smashes into the water without warning. Ellen stands on the pier, murder in her eyes, and grunts as the young man splashes about trying to find the ladder to freedom.

"Howdy boss," Shaw says happily, acting like nothing has happened. "Glad you could make it."

"Whose idea?" she says, her voice filled with curiosity instead of anger.

With a groan, Shaw gets to his feet and begins throwing tactical bags onto the deck of the small schooner. "Both of us. Gotta have some fun in this hole."

Ellen turns as each bag thuds heavily onto the deck and she studies the small vessel. "Get him out of the water."

Christopher finds a length of rope and tosses it into the water. Lloyd thrashes over to it, his hands trying to grab the now slippery material. "Do I need to get one of these fine gents to fish you out?"

Lloyd is panting heavily as he finally grabs the rope and slowly pulls himself up, all the while coughing and spluttering.

"Stop," Ellen's voice freezes Shaw who turns slowly. "It won't do."

"Huh?" Shaw says, not fully comprehending.

The woman points in the direction of the water and the large man follows. His eyes widen slightly at the sight of the waves and the dark clouds forming. "Ah," is all he can say.

Ellen nods, "We're going to need a bigger boat."

"Is that a Jaws reference?" Lloyd says with a slight shiver.

Their boss shakes her head firmly. "Shut up." She looks at Shaw and Christopher, "Get us a bigger boat, something that'll stay afloat."

"That's going to cost extra," Christopher says.

"I don't care," she says. "We have limited time to get to the island, so stop wasting it and get working."

The two men don't bother arguing; instead they turn and walk away, looking for the next best thing. Ellen looks at the drenched man and shakes her head. "You ready for this?"

Lloyd nods though with the shivering it looks like he isn't sure about what he has signed up for. Ellen notices this and places a reassuring hand on his wet shoulder. "No matter what happens, we are on the side of right. It doesn't matter what the animal is, we will do everything we can to save them."

"Even kill?"

#

"What a surprise," James McTiernan says as yet another 'system failure' warning message pops up on one of the multitude of monitors in Security Control. Last count this was the fiftieth warning to appear in the last hour and it probably will be the fiftieth time S&P will tell him, "We're on it," and then promptly ignore everything except what Pryke says. He rubs his face as monotonous beeps sounds loudly. "What is it now?"

JR Handley casually looks to the monitor on his console and chuckles. "It's that woman...Mako something or other." McTiernan raises an eyebrow and follows the gaze to the main entrance. The metal sliding door is opened with a combination of ID card, retinal scanning and voice recognition; no way are they going to let just anyone enter his domain. "Must be having trouble with the system," Handley says with a shrug.

Mako Ikari stands outside and is getting frustrated with the people staring at her from inside the hi-tech room. It's rare for her to make the trip from Asset Containment to Security but so far the only times has been when the data transfer systems have failed. She taps on the bullet proof glass and waves.

McTiernan shakes his head and slowly gets up. He straightens his uniform with a sharp pull that reminds his people of Captain Picard from 'Star Trek Next Generation', though none would ever say so. It takes the man seven large steps to make it to the door. He presses his left thumb to the reader and the door slides open with a faint whoosh. Mako bows her head in thanks before looking up at the man. "What can I do for you Miss Ikari?"

She bristles at the lack of Professor but tries to ignore it. "The message system is on the blink again." McTiernan raises an eyebrow at her, waiting for the next part. "Well," she sighs "I've got all of the data on the Cat 5." Mako holds out a large manila folder with the words CATEGORY 5 - CODENAME 'ISHIRO' written on the front.

"Ishiro?" McTiernan asks with a chuckle.

Mako nods. "We always give them names. Can you try to send it to the other departments and to Mister Pryke?"

"Naturally," the ex-military man says as the small Japanese woman turns and walks away. McTiernan shakes his head as the doors close behind him, his eyes staring at the file and he sighs. "Winder, get in touch with S&P once again and find out what is going on with the systems. Please." He doesn't bother looking at the man as he walks into his office. The moment he lands in the seat the file is open and McTiernan's eyes scan the pages rapidly. He won't admit it but like everyone else James McTiernan is curious about the Category 5 Kaiju, what can it do? How does it look?

Size - 250 meters tall.

Weight - 160,000 tonnes.

Abilities - X-Ray from eyes, high amounts of radiation, possible wings forming, no signs of atomic breath capabilities.

When he gets to the section for 'Description' there is nothing but a hand written note: SEE PHOTOS. Which is what he does and as he looks at each photo, he cannot believe the amount of new problems that the A.R. Team has brought them. Due to the sheer size of the thing, the photos only show sections but the image that McTiernan gets in his mind's eye is enough to make him drop them; the claws on the four toed feet are larger than buses and look like they could tear a tank in half easily, the muscular legs are full of power and the man has no doubt that it could get across the USA within two hours. But what gives him the chills is the head. It looks just like a Rottweiler's head, the same shape and width but it is missing certain things; such as the floppy ears and the splotches of brown fur, in fact the entire body is covered in nothing but leather and armour plating. McTiernan wonders what it would take to bring the creature down quickly but his mind goes blank.

"We are truly FUBAR'd," he mutters, using the old lingo. He grabs his phone and finds the number for Pryke's direct line.

"James!" Pryke's voice is jovial. "Are you getting ready to come and say Hi to our guests?"

"No...Wait, what?" McTiernan didn't agree to that. "No, Mister Pryke I've got the breakdown of the Cat 5. Can you talk?"

"Certainly m'boy! Our guests are just getting comfortable and cleaned up." His voice is slightly slurred which means he's already cracked open a bottle of Glenlivet 30 years old. "So, the Cat 5 eh? What do we call the tyke?"

McTiernan rubs the bridge of his nose. "That little tyke is bigger than the one that attacked Tokyo."

"Wow! So more than 150 meters?"

"Yes. At least 250 and they haven't figured out all of its abilities. Which has me worried."

Pryke laughs. "That's your job James. So, what's his name?"

"Ishiro," McTiernan says softly. There is something about the name that gives him the same feeling he used to get just before an operation; a mixture of fear, nervous excitement and that knowing idea of ensuing chaos. He loves it and hates it at the same time.

"Ishiro," Pryke rolls the word around his mouth. "I like it! When can he be ready for a show?"

"No idea Mister Pryke--"

"--Gideon."

You can keep telling me that, McTiernan thinks as he says, "Mister Pryke, looking at this report I don't think that Ishiro is a prime candidate for the park--"

"--Pish tosh! We have the best people and Mako knows what she's doing!" Pryke's voice leaves no room for argument. "Now, when can I expect you and our expert for lunch?"

McTiernan steps outside his office and throws the file down onto the console in front of Handley. "Get this onto the system and sent to everyone."

"James?"

A sigh comes from the Head of Security and James McTiernan knows better than to try and argue. "I'll pick up Miss Ikari and head on down to the restaurant."

"Bully!" and without another word the owner of Kaiju World hangs up.

McTiernan stares at the main screen and watches the various security camera feeds cycle through. His eyes focus while his mind wanders; he knows for a fact that there is no way they can contain Ishiro if it decides to go on a rampage...*That's the last thing we need,* he thinks. *If that happens who knows what the other Kaijus will do or how we can keep everything under control.* He looks at the majority of his team. Every man and woman in this room are the best and his most trusted, each one perfectly trained and willing to do whatever it takes to finish the job, no matter the cost. *We could call Tokyo for a nuke,* he muses then quickly pushes that idea away. He knows that not only would the Japanese government never agree to it but also Gideon Pryke would have a coronary even contemplating the idea. *Gideon Pryke...*

"I'll be back later," he says, then turns and exits without another word.

#

"Gentlemen!" Pryke says cheerfully as each of the investors walk down the grand staircase in the middle of the hotel/guest resort. "I hope you are refreshed and ready for a delicious meal before setting out on the first ever tour of Kaiju World." His smile says it all; you better be ready.

"Are you married to the name?" Tull says softly.

Pryke blinks, "Huh?"

Tull nods as he casually pushes his glasses up the bridge of his nose. "Yes. The name, 'Kaiju World'. Don't you think it sounds like...Oh, I don't know, like something from a bad TV movie?" He looks around at his partners, hoping for backup. He has never been good at confronting the eccentric billionaire but the name is important to the man.

"Interesting," Pryke says with complete disinterest. "We'll come back to that." His eyes scan the faces of the men and he claps his hands excitedly. "Are there any other questions?"

Hands hit the air and Gideon Pryke smiles in the exact same way that a child with a secret to tell does. "Follow me gentlemen and all shall be revealed."

He takes off at a brisk walk that forces the five men to jog to keep up with him. Walking around the staircase, Gideon Pryke pushes on two large wooden doors with ornate carvings in them, the shapes are of monsters and various demonic looking animals. Inside they find themselves in a gigantic conference room. The lines and flow is definitely reminiscent of a Japanese temple, there is a small waterfall that provides a soothing counterpoint to whatever is going to be discussed. Along the circular table are bonsai trees and the entire room is peaceful.

"Gentlemen, take your seats," Pryke says with a grand sweeping of his arm.

"Why should we?" Emmerich says suspiciously.

Pryke chuckles, "You don't have to, but trust me, you'll want to." There is something about his voice that makes each of the powerful men sit down. Pryke watches and his smile says it all; hold onto your butts. Walking over to a large panel that has a stylistic piece of art on it, he gestures at it grandly. "I had this commissioned by one of the best Japanese artists. Do you know what it is?" Of course they don't and Pryke would have been surprised if they did. Outside of their world each man has no interest in other cultures.

Each man looks at the painting; the brush strokes are fluid and the parchment mixed with the paint has an amazing level of contrast that is at the same time beautiful and horrific. The painting shows the destruction of Tokyo city, buildings are being toppled, people stomped and burning from flames. The actual creature stands on the left side of the painting and towers over the buildings. Pryke smiles at it in admiration, "This was the very first Kaiju to ever be discovered on Earth, and it was gloriously terrible."

"How can you say that?" Crichton is repulsed by the joy Pryke shows. "Millions were killed."

"Yes!" Pryke says with a snap of the fingers. "They were killed, but that is life. And life is terrible and glorious." He leans against the wall smugly. "Which is why we love horror movies, ghost stories and anything that scares us," he taps the canvas. "Ten years ago I saw the carnage and my charity helped with the reconstruction. Then the idea came to me, how could I take this naturally occurring phenomenon and make it so that we need not be scared?"

"A theme park?" Beacham scoffs.

Gideon Pryke nods. "Yes. Just like Sean Drummond's Dino Park but instead of cloned monsters masquerading as dinosaurs we would have the real deal. The paying public could get up close and see that these monsters are nothing more than animals. And unlike Drummond's house of horrors I would not cut corners or rush to open."

Winston nods, "Which is why it has taken you so long?"

Pryke smiles, "That brings us to now. In two weeks, we shall open and already the first month has sold out." He chuckles. "You'll make your investment back within five months."

Emmerich stands "Enough of the sales talk! Show us why we are here."

A man who has never been able to handle demands, Pryke stares at Emmerich, his face unreadable. Then, "Certainly." He taps a small square wooden panel right next to the frame and it pops open, the owner of the park presses a button and the entire room lurches sharply.

The five investors grab their chair arms tightly and stare at the room, hoping that it is not an earthquake. There is a hydraulics sound which is followed by the room beginning to move.

"Drummond's plan was to have the biggest and most impressive dinosaurs roaming his park. Think T-Rex, Apatosaurus, Brachiosaurs and any others that you can think of. Here? Everything is impressive, the biggest and the best. Nothing small and cute for the children because they don't want cute. More teeth, more power, more everything," Pryke says with grandeur as the lights dim. "What do earthquakes, tsunamis and volcanoes all have in common? Humans cannot do anything to stop them." He speaks faster and faster as light begins to fill the room. "But what if we could stop the full power of nature? Capture it? Harness it? Make it our slaves? That is the question that we, here at Kaiju World have answered."

He ignores the snicker from Tull and pushes on, "Gentlemen, this is the future of theme parks. This is Kaiju World!"

The men gasp as the meeting room clears the building and light floods in. The room is completely surrounded by the plains of the island. The plants, trees and view are awe-inspiring. But what sucks the air out of the room are the three gigantic monsters roaming the area. Each one is completely different to the last. A smooth sphere rolls past and the men all clamour to see it better.

Pryke looks at it happily, "That's Anno, one of the weaker ones." He walks over and stands next to them. "So, why have other theme parks trying to corner the extreme market all failed?"

"They don't have these," Beacham sighs.

Anno, the sphere stops and it seems to turn. A gigantic eye slit opens in the middle and the blood-red iris stares at the men behind the barrier. It roars and slams into the room. The men scream and leap back as the Kaiju splits in two; the gigantic mouth filled with teeth tries to bite into the meeting room.

"Don't worry," Pryke says cheerfully as the men get to see the massive scaly tongue trying to grip the smooth Perspex. "All of our buildings have been completely reinforced to survive everything these beasties can throw at us."

After a few seconds more, Anno growls then rolls away again. The men cannot believe it, for their entire lives they have spent it mostly in the safety of the boardroom. Now they are staring death in the face and they love it!

His point made, Gideon Pryke claps his hands and says, "Any questions?"

#

"I've been looking forward to this," Dutch says as he pops open the cold beer and takes a long gulp. The moment the beverage leaves his lips, he releases a long, "Ahhhhh."

Unlike Security, Containment or the main control area, the Asset Recruitment Team or ART for short, have their own separate little hole-in-the-wall that they call home. Located out in the middle of the island, the bungalow is hidden nicely in the middle of a forest that is too thick for the monsters to get through. And though it is separate to the main compound, Dutch and his team have no problem with moving across the island thanks to a monorail system and underground tunnels.

The large man looks around and smiles; they've been cooped up together for almost five years and yet every time he sees them all together, Johann, Roxie and Lawrence, Dutch feels like he is home. Right now they are getting ready to eat and it's Lawrence's turn to cook.

"Here ya go," his deep voice booms. "Lasagne." He puts down on the table a large casserole dish that is over-filled with steaming hot pasta.

"Wow," Roxie says. "That looks like the dog's bollocks!"

"How many times," Johann laughs, "have I told you to use proper English. Not that Australian bastardization."

Dutch can't help but join in the laughter. He is always glad to be back after a hunting expedition. But, part of him knows that sooner rather than later, they'll get the call to pack up and head out for the next recruitment. His eyes watch as Lawrence slices up the pasta and begins serving it. "I'll get the drinks," he says, standing with ease.

Before anyone can stop him, he goes over to the small wine cooler and opens it. His finger slides down the cool bottles until he finds the perfect one.

"Not the Rosé," Roxie shouts from behind.

"I know," Dutch shouts back as he grabs a bottle of Leeuwin Estate Art Series Chardonnay. He knows the others aren't that fond of whites, but it is his favourite. As he turns back and looks for the cork-screw, his phone starts to vibrate.

"No phones at dinner!" Johann sneers.

"Yeah!" Lawrence joins. "I've been slaving away all day for you cretins."

"Fuck you," Roxie punches Lawrence's arm. "Only cretin here is Pryke." That gets the laugh.

"That's our boss," Dutch says seriously. The others look at him like he is crazy then nod when he holds up the phone. Placing the bottle on the table next to Roxie he steps away. "Dutch here," he answers.

"Dutch!" it's Pryke. "Glad that you've settled in. Listen--"

"--No Gideon. Give us a week at least."

"M'boy! You really need to listen to a whole sentence," Pryke sounds exuberant. "I just need you to come down at lunch and tell our guests about your job and some war stories."

Before Dutch can answer, the phone clicks and he can only hear the dial tone. Looking up at the meal before him, Dutch sighs. "I'm needed for some dog and pony show."

"What?! You're not available."

Dutch stands there, his mind weighing the pros and cons; on the one hand they have been working overtime to get the Category 5 brought back before the visit. But, Pryke was notorious for not accepting no's. This made him a pain to deal with. *But,* he thinks, *if I do this then maybe we can get some much needed holidays. Or at least a month's extra pay.* He nods, then walks past them, for the front door. "Enjoy the meal," he says quietly.

Roxie speaks around a mouthful of food, "Cut the tall poppy down!"

Dutch waves as he grabs a heavy jacket and opens the door, the storm clouds are thick and dark and he doesn't like their chances of no rain. With a sigh, Dutch steps outside his sanctuary. He has plenty of time before lunch, but he decides to get a wriggle on just so he can check out the Cat 5 and make sure it is behaving.

CHAPTER FIVE

"Where the hell did you find these?"

"How the hell?"

"Are you out of your fucking mind?"

Tull, Beacham and Emmerich all repeat their questions quickly and with a growing amount of trepidation. It's obvious to Gideon Pryke that they are incapable of processing the idea of the gigantic monstrous creatures. He sighs and claps his hands loudly to get the five men's attention, "Gentlemen." He presses the side panel button and slowly the room begins to rise back up into the rest of the compound. "If you'll follow me, everything will be explained to you." Pryke doesn't wait for an answer; turning he walks over and just as the room clicks into place he swings open the large doors.

"Was that real?" Tull mutters to the other four men. "I mean, can those things be...?" he leaves the question hanging in the air.

Winston nods, "As real as you or I."

"Umm," Beacham points to the open door. "Shouldn't we?"

They take off at a run, hoping to catch up with their host and now favourite client. Their voices echo as they shout, "Pryke! Wait! Pryke!"

All make it out the door except for Emmerich whose eyes have not left the incredible sight. A small smile creeps across his face and the German thinks, *What else can they be used for?* Before turning and hurrying to catch up to the others.

"Ah, thought you'd gotten lost," Pryke says with a chuckle. "Or eaten!" He laughs as the five men stare at him. This was the reaction he'd been hoping for and the man is delighted at his guest's faces. Casually he checks his watch. "Hmmm." A look of consternation crosses his face,

"Lunch is still a couple of hours away...What to do, eh?"

Emmerich raises his hand. "Can we see more?"

Gideon Pryke beams, his teeth showing as his eyes light up. "I thought you'd never ask," but of course he did. So far everyone who has seen the monsters has always had the same reaction: more. "Right, this way gentlemen." Pryke leads the way, a bounce in his step that wasn't there before.

"Where'd they come from?"

Pryke turns and glances at Crichton. "We don't rightly know. Oh of course we do have theories. But that's all they are, wild and unfounded assumptions. Our resident expert, Mako Ikari, can explain it all to you. But what I can tell you," he says cheerfully, "is that it's a jolly good show trying to round up the buggers."

The way he says it makes the others laugh. It's a nervous mixed with excitement laugh and to Pryke he's got them lock stock and barrel. As they continue walking, he begins to think about how much to tell them. That's been his problem with most of his endeavours, when it comes to the science, Gideon Pryke just doesn't give a damn. It bores him to death. Give him an audience and something to sell?

Pure gold.

"...dollars and they'll pay," Emmerich's voice brings Pryke back. "What sort of merchandise are you preparing?"

Pryke blinks, "Merchandising? You mean toys?"

"You want to try scanning one of those things," the gruff voice startles the five men, "then by all means. Be my guest."

"Ah, this is our head of Asset Recruitment, Charles Dutch." Pryke is happy for the extra help.

Dutch nods curtly at the five men while trying to ignore the use of his full name. "They may look cuddly and perfect for kids," he continues, "but make one of these things angry and a city is gone." It's obvious that he doesn't care for any of these men and the feeling is definitely mutual.

"Mister Dutch," Tull says, "maybe you don't understand how business works--"

"--Okay," the large man says, speaking over the top of Tull. "Come with me." He gives a curt nod to Pryke who looks like he could go for some popcorn right now.

The investors watch him stride down the hallway and disappear around a corner. "Who is that?" Winston rumbles.

"Just the man who captures our attractions...Shall we?"

#

43

"What's that?"

"Huh?"

Handley stares at Winder who does nothing but grin. "Check your screen."

Winder casually stretches then glances at his screen. A frown creases his brow and he scratches his neck. "What the..?"

JR Handley nods, "Do you think we ought to alert him?"

Chris Winder checks the settings of his station. The small blip on the screen is closing in, moving slowly towards the mass that is Maikeru Island. It shouldn't be there. "Could it be a Kaiju?"

Handley shakes his head. "Too small." The implication of what it could be makes both men gulp nervously. Around them the other members of the Security Team are busy taking care of their own duties. No one else has noticed the discrepancy but soon it would happen--

"Whatcha looking at?"

"Pipe down Homer!" Winder snaps at Simpson. The new guy has a habit of sneaking up on people which, in a room full of ex-military is an extremely stupid thing to do.

"Sorry," Simpson says, looking at the screen. "That's a boat."

Handley and Winder stare at the youngish man in surprise. "How the fuck do you know that?"

Simpson puffs up with pride. "Navy. First thing you learn is how to spot a boat by the speed."

"Oh, so you did learn something else apart from the fun of glory holes?"

The young man is about to open his mouth to retort when Donna Mixon calls out, "Who the fuck isn't paying attention to their fucking cunt screens?"

All bodies in the Control Room stop moving. There are two rules that are completely unbreakable for Security; 1) Don't mention any past missions or conflicts. 2) Never mess with 'Mad' Mixon. Even McTiernan is afraid of the ex-Sargent Major, but he'll never admit it. Mixon is short but built to kill. She was the first McTiernan hired and whenever he isn't around 'Mad' Mixon is in charge.

"Sorry Donna," Winder says as he shoves Simpson towards his own station.

"Shove your sorry up your cloaca," she snarls. For as long as anyone can remember, Mixon has had a very extensive vocabulary at her disposal. "Why am I getting alerts about a boat?"

Handley speaks up, trying to calm her, "Are you sure it's a boat? No disrespect."

"Who pulled the cock out of your ass?" Mixon spits. "You two cumsponges need to do your job." She pauses for a moment. Then, "Or, I'll do it for you." Her threat lands hard as she turns back to her own screen. A few seconds later the others follow, going back to their own jobs.

Winder and Handley have the exact same look and thought; who's going to tell McTiernan? As Handley opens his mouth Winder butts in, "I'll alert A.R. Team."

"Okay, then...Wait...What?"

Handley smiles. "That's a good man! McTiernan's gonna take the news just fine." He turns back to his screen and begins compiling the message. As he clicks the send button, Winder punches his shoulder, "Hey!"

"You dick," Winder says. "We should follow procedures and check with the mainland."

The other man blinks. "Why didn't we think of that in the first place?"

"Because you're a couple of mindless cum-guzzlers," Mixon's voice echoes across the room.

The two men choose to ignore her and focus on the problem at hand. "You prime the message to McTiernan. I'll call Tokyo."

Winder opens his mouth but Handley is already on the phone. He dials a number then waits patiently for an answer, tapping his fingers rhythmically on the table top, "Have you done it?" Handley holds up a hand, stopping Winder talking. "Hai, koreha Maikeru airandodesu..." He blinks listening to the voice on the other end of the phone. "Really?" Handley switches to English with a sigh. "Thank you...What..? Yes my accent is terrible." He laughs but rolls his eyes at Winder. "Listen," he continues, "we have a blip on our radar and was curious if any chartered boats have left--" He stops again, listening once more. "Oh, okay. Are you sure..? Okay, thank you. Sayonara." Handley hangs up then looks at Winder with a slight shake of his head.

"What?"

"They say," Handley begins as his eyes dart around, "that there hasn't been any that have chartered their course near us, or past us. In fact, the last boat to have its course entered as here was the boss' own yacht."

"Shit," Winder has a sinking feeling and quickly wipes his brow. "What if it's a Kaiju?"

"Then you two can quit being pussies and grow some balls," Mixon says.

Handley and Winder look at each other, their expressions are one of bemusement. "How does she do that?"

Handley shakes his head saying, "No clue...Just let the boss know." He turns away, ignoring Winder's protests as he types up a message then sends it.

#

"Fuck," James McTiernan mutters to himself as he rereads the message once more. This is the last thing they need, some tourist stumbling across the island and running into one of the beasts. Even the Category 1s can be problematic; most of the Kaijus have fire, laser or gas breath that can destroy a building easily. *What a fucking nightmare!*

The lift pings and shudders as the breaks lock in place. McTiernan stares at his phone and his brow furrows. *Why are they sending A.R. Team?* A breach is his jurisdiction; the only time A.R. Team is called in is when a Kaiju escapes... Quickly he pulls up the map of the island and checks the coordinates. He nods, now understanding; A.R. Team's bungalow is located on the western part of the island and the blip is south-west. *They'll be quicker*, he thinks.

The doors slide open with a slight sigh and McTiernan hides his surprise as Pryke, the five guests and Dutch shuffle into the cramped space. Gideon Pryke is all smiles, "Ah what a happy accident this is. This, gents, is the man in charge of maintaining peace and order for the park, James McTiernan."

McTiernan nods politely and pushes his way over to Dutch. Once again the doors sigh shut and the transport begins moving again. "Here," he says, showing the bear of a man the phone.

Dutch's eyes take the message in quickly and he nods. "They won't move."

"They better," McTiernan speaks just above a whisper.

"Nope," the two men keep their eyes forward as Pryke explains how the different departments are connected. It's polite chit-chat, nothing more. Dutch looks bored as he repeats, "Nope. Nothing will shift them."

"It could be anything," McTiernan says. "A boat. Terrorists." Dutch laughs at that. "Or," McTiernan pushes on, "a Kaiju."

Some of the investors turn their heads slightly at the word. Both McTiernan and Dutch shake their heads and smile reassuringly. The heads turn back and Dutch snarls softly, "Watch your mouth."

"Get my point?" McTiernan ignores the threatening tone.

Dutch is silent as the lift continues its journey. His shoulders slump forward slightly as he nods, "I'll get them on it."

"Much obliged," McTiernan's thanks is genuine. "How's the show going?"

"They need a lesson in humility."

"And you're the man to give it."

Dutch's smile is cruel; the man has trouble suffering fools or arrogance. They turn their attention back to their employer. "It's all geothermal. No need for a power plant, just a couple of turbines and unlimited renewable energy. Keeps the expenses down," Pryke finishes just as the lift pings and the doors open again.

One by one they pile out and McTiernan taps Dutch's shoulders. "After the lesson, get with your team. I'll take care of Pryke."

Dutch looks slightly confused, but he nods anyway then steps out. McTiernan watches as he roughly shoves the soft men aside. He follows after sending a confirmation message.

Mako Ikari is already waiting for the group, she presses her hands against her hips in a power stance and wears an unimpressed expression. Obviously she's not finished her work with the Category 5, Ishiro. As both Dutch and McTiernan get closer they can see Pryke gently push the woman into the fray, the investors swarming her, roughly shaking her hand and bombarding the attractive woman with questions. Poor Mako is in over her head.

"Vultures," Dutch murmurs.

McTiernan nods. "Almost as bad as zoomies." Both men laugh and then walk over, McTiernan goes straight to Pryke and gently pulls him to the side. "What is it James?"

"This is just a courtesy," McTiernan says softly. "We might have a potential situation."

"Don't be telling me pork pies!" Pryke's original accent comes out in full force.

"It's okay," McTiernan's voice is all reassuring. "Dutch and his team are going to handle it."

Pryke has the exact same look as someone having a heart attack. His eyes bulge and a vein in his neck looks close to exploding. McTiernan stays quiet, he knows better than to say anything but still, "Not in front of the guests."

That does the trick and Pryke takes a deep breath. Slowly he exhales, letting the air out with a tiny whooshing sound. Looking a more human colour, the owner of Kaiju World asks, "Why aren't you sending your own boys?"

Dutch answers, "We're better equipped for any eventualities." An expert at recovery, Pryke smiles just for the sake of the investors and says, "Bully!" even though the joviality is clearly forced. The Head of A.R. Team looks at the small group of people. "C'mon."

Mako steps forward and with a slight bow begins talking. "Please follow me." They start walking with Dutch at the lead, followed by Mako and then the rest. "We're about to enter Containment. This is where we do all of our tests and experiments on the Kaijus. Before entering you will all have to pass through decontamination."

"Why? What's the worst that can happen?" Beacham asks.

A smile crosses Mako's face. "You'd be perfectly fine. Until the bacteria comes into contact with your skin."

A blink from the younger businessman. "Then?"

"One of the most virulent diseases ever seen will attack all your body's systems. The symptoms are similar to those of rabies, syphilis and anthrax. You'll be dead in twenty-four hours after first contact." Mako stares at the gathered men, a pleasant smile on her face. "But they will be the most excruciating twenty-four hours of your life, guaranteed."

The five men are dumbfounded at the mixture of problems they can get. Beacham is shaking with fright; Tull is expressionless while Emmerich looks utterly confused. Crichton and Winston are not sure whether to laugh or cry.

"Mako," Pryke's voice has the tone of a disapproving father. "Play nice."

A pout appears then just as quickly vanishes as Mako Ikari says, "My apologies." She is completely formal and bows again slightly. "I meant no disrespect. It was just a joke."

"Oh!" Crichton laughs and soon the others join in, though Beacham and Tull just chuckle.

"No harm," Winston says. "What would happen?"

The woman half-smiles. "Nothing. You'd be totally fine. But our boys?" Mako sighs, "When we first get them they have to get...acclimated to us." A distant look comes across her face as a memory hits her.

"So," Emmerich starts, "what does happen?"

"That," Dutch says with a small head gesture.

As they've been walking and talking, none of the investors have noticed the large glass panels that reveal an impressive laboratory. Inside it are technicians and scientists who are all busy with studying, moving and dissecting slabs of meat, bone, masses of tissues and organs. At least the investors hope they are organs for each one is misshapen or oddly coloured with hard ridges and what can only be called teeth.

A technician uses large nasty looking tongs to lift up one of the oversized organs, it tears and sludge oozes out splattering down onto the tiles. Pryke bangs on the thick glass. "Careful you fool!"

The technician doesn't look up as he is quickly helped by others. As one unit they use mops to clean up most of the goo which is then dropped into a large barrel, after that high-powered hoses are used to wash away any and all remaining residue. More mops are then used to finish cleaning up, and then all of it is promptly deposited into the same barrel which is sealed and then rolled away.

"Impressive response time," Emmerich admits with a small degree of admiration.

Mako nods and they continue walking. "Would you believe that nearly all of them have a different physiology? Unlike humans, dogs or even fish, which all have similar structures, the Kaiju are all completely different. Some are like reptiles, cold blooded while others could be descended from birds or marsupials." She is talking excitedly and having the time of her life.

"So, where do they come from?" Crichton asks as they approach large security doors.

"We don't know," Mako says honestly. "It could be from another world, dimension or even remnants of some long thought extinct species. There was even some discussion about how they could be scientific experiments...Perhaps human cloning or genetic splicing that went horribly wrong." The doors open silently and Mako Ikari steps into the decontamination chamber. "Please."

#

"Steady!" Ellen Scott shouts at Lloyd Behm as he fights with the helm. The young man smiles sheepishly then focuses on not running aground. "Where'd you find him?" Ellen asks Christopher Michael.

The midget shakes his head. "You said find a true believer."

Ellen blinks then grabs the railing, steadying herself. The journey from Tokyo harbor had been rougher than they had expected, luckily though their leader had the foresight to change boats. If they had stayed with the original chartered vessel they surely would have capsized by now. As it stands, the south-western landing site is visible. But so are the rocks and coral reefs.

The boat smacks and then bounces off one of the medium sized rocks and Lloyd shouts, "Sorry!"

Ellen shakes her head, "How did we not know about these damn rocks?"

A slightly odd-accented voice says, "All of the recon was done during high-tide." Jeremy Smith stares at the woman, his dark eyes unblinking, giving him the appearance of an alien. His long dark braided hair looks at odds with the rest of his outfit; khakis and a flak jacket.

The blonde's eyes bulge in disbelief. "Wait...You're telling me that all of our planning has been done--"

"--Hang on!"

"Done solely in daylight?"

"Hang on to something!" Lloyd calls again then quickly drops behind the helm.

Ellen turns, ready to throw the new guy overboard when with a lurching shake and an unholy scraping sound the boat shudders to a halt. The sudden stop throws everyone that is not Lloyd forward. "Here we are," he says cheerfully looking at his handy-work.

The prow of the boat is wedged up and deep in the dry sand of the picturesque beach. The sand itself is bright, almost totally white. Nearly all of the beaches on the island are covered in the same fine grains. About a hundred meters or so up the beach is a lush green forest. It's not a gradual change of environment but a hard sudden appearance. The foliage is dense and looks almost like it has been sculpted to be this way. *They don't want us getting in,* Ellen thinks as her eyes take in the sight, *or want to keep something from escaping.*

"Move it or lose it," Rick Shaw says, using his bulk to push the woman aside. He is carrying tactical bags and tosses them down to Christopher who catches it easily then throws it up the surf to Jeremy who is making a pile of their equipment. Each one lands on the sand with a dull thud.

None of them says anything as Ellen goes over to Lloyd and roughly grabs him by the neck. He squeaks as she speaks, "Are you actively trying to get us caught? Or is it just natural stupidity?"

Lloyd slaps her hand, trying to get her to let go as his face turns blue while he struggles to breathe. The woman relaxes her grip just enough for the man to gasp for air. Once the colour returns, he speaks, "I told you to hold on."

Ellen blinks, expecting more and when she realises that there is nothing else, a smile appears on her pale face. "That you did...Hold. On."

Lloyd Behm yelps as he sails over the side and lands in the cool aqua water with a loud splash mixed with a thud. Ellen leans over and stares at the four men. "You've got five minutes to get everything unloaded."

#

The investors cough and splutter, trying to get rid of the aftertaste of the decontamination spray. Only Dutch, Mako, Pryke and McTiernan are unfazed by the experience. As the hidden fans pull the remnants out of the chamber, Mako says, "We have refreshments outside."

Once the security doors open, the five men run over to a metal table with a large tray on top. Upon it are tall glasses of water that are quickly devoured en masse. The four park workers walk over and Dutch clears his throat, a deep rumble that freezes the men. "Let's move," the commanding tone works perfectly and the investors put the glasses down. The head of A.R. Team turns on his foot and sets off. Everyone, save for McTiernan, hurries to catch up.

"What's the plan?" Emmerich demands. "We're not cattle, you know!"

Dutch stops as the others murmur similar sentiments. His eyes are hard and with his imposing build the powerful businessmen cower slightly. Dutch smiles as he speaks, "This is the danger. Miss Ikari?"

They are standing before another large shuttered room. There are no signs or markings but Mako and Dutch know exactly where they are. Taking her cue, the Kaiju expert scans her ID card in a small wall-mounted reader and sirens begin flashing as the annoying whine deafens them. Clamping their hands to their ears the investors glare at Mako. As the lights dim, the shutters begin to roll up. "You wanted to see one up close," Dutch barks, his voice easily heard over the wailing klaxons. "You got it."

Mouths drop open as the frightened voices whimper, "Dear God." And, "Help us."

"Say hello," Mako says, "to Ishiro."

Even Gideon Pryke, the man who has seen charging a tiger up close and wrestled bears for fun is forced to whimper, "Amazing!"

The giant eye shifts slightly, the massive muscles pulsing as it moves the ocular organ, focusing on the nine people. A feeling of absolute terror overtakes them and as the pupil dilates, the shutters close, shielding the people from the terrible eye.

Dutch turns and says, "Enjoy the rest of your stay." Then he walks, disappearing around a corner.

Pryke steps forward, taking the lead. "Well...How about a little break while Mako does some minor surgery? Oh it's nothing invasive, just implanting our security measures." Not waiting for an answer, Pryke and McTiernan lead the stunned men over to a small lounge area. It looks similar to a beach bar found in the Bahamas; wicker chairs, a beach sound-scape playing and tiki glasses everywhere.

"Now this is better," Beacham says as he grabs a tall scotch. The others follow suit and soon the five money men are laughing and acting like what they had just seen, never happened.

"A word James," Pryke says then leads McTiernan to a small alcove.

"Yes Gideon?"

The older man throws his Panama hat onto a chair while taking a deep breath. When he looks at the Head of Security, all trace of joviality is gone. What remains is cruel and shrewd, "What was that all about?"

McTiernan smiles ever-so-slightly, he is better with direct questioning. "I'm not sure I know what you mean."

"Can it! Dutch and his little show back there, what was the point?"

"Sir?" McTiernan goes back to his army days.

Pryke senses this and pushes the advantage. "You better answer me. Am I not your commanding officer?"

"Sir!" McTiernan stands erect as he speaks. "Dutch wanted to teach the guests a lesson in humility. That is all."

"And you didn't think to stop him?" Behind them the investors are getting rowdy. Pryke clears his throat. "Just do your job and pray they love the tour."

Before McTiernan can answer, Pryke grabs his hat, fixes a smile to his face and then goes over to the five drinking men saying, "Better slow down! There's still lunch and then the tour proper."

James McTiernan watches the group of men and thinks, *This is why I stay away.* Since going into the private sector he has learned one very important lesson; people are complete assholes. He's known it all his life but his COs and squad mates were decent and enjoyed a laugh. But civilians? Selfish, rude, crude and totally without a sense of unit. *It's a dog eat dog world,* he reminds himself.

"Mister Pryke," Mako's voice echoes in the lounge from a series of speakers that are strategically mounted in the walls and ceilings. "We're ready here."

"Bully!" Pryke says with a clap. "Gentlemen, how about a show?"

"Girls?!" Tull slurs slightly as he flops into one of the wicker seats.

"Oh heaven's no. Not until tonight," Pryke says with a sly wink.

The man could be an Oscar winner, McTiernan thinks as he watches the philanthropist.

Pryke's eyes never leaves the other men as they slump into the comfy chairs. "So, to save those of you with weak constitutions we'll be viewing the procedures via a live feed." As if on cue a large screen slowly lights up. On it they can see Mako and some of the technicians walking around a scaly landscape. "What our dear Mako is going to do," he continues, "is really nothing more than tagging the beast. Just like we do with dogs and cats. This way Security and A.R. Team can track it all over the island to within ten meters."

"Oh," Crichton says softly as Mako and her team begin the process of cutting at the thick flesh. They use a process of lasers, chainsaws and heavy machetes; its hide is that thick.

"Don't worry," Pryke says as the men squirm and flinch in their seats. "The animal is completely anesthetized and unaware of what's happening to it."

On the screen, as Mako does her job, orange blood seeps and oozes from the giant veins that surround the bright purple flesh. Ishiro is knocked out and periodically shifts and rumbles. A crane begins to lower a blinking probe that is the size of a man. "That's our tracker," Pryke continues as they start to push the device into place. "They did try experimenting with smaller models but for some reason the muscles had this annoying habit of crushing them."

"Spare no expenses," Tull mutters with a childish laugh.

Pryke ignores the comment and goes to open his mouth when Emmerich gets to his feet. "Yes?"

"This is all wonderful," the German says with an air of superiority. "But, how do we know that this idea to use these...monsters as attractions is going to be as profitable as you say?"

Pryke smiles as he talks. "What a valid question! Well, to answer that and any others you may have...Let's crack on!"

CHAPTER SIX

"What's our position?" Ellen Scott asks softly as the small band crouches in the forest below a large tree. It hadn't taken them long to unload and perform a quick count. In total they have ten pounds of C4 plastic explosives, a couple of small calibre handguns, two shotguns with plenty of ammunition and enough rations to last a week. Under the branches and leaves the entire landscape has a strange alien quality to it, as if the plants were created from different species and spliced together. The smells are unlike regular jungle smells, no sweet air or that hint of moisture, but there is a very distinct scent of musk and something artificial, like there is perfume being pumped all around them.

Jeremy checks the map and quickly traces a few different routes with his finger. He nods. "Depending on how quickly you want to do this, either three hours hiking or five."

"What's the difference?" Rick Shaw asks, grabbing the map. He holds it up to the light and squints, studying the topographical lines. "Either way we're gonna get dirty."

The large man takes back the map gently so as to not tear it and says, "Do you know what's waiting for us?" Jeremy's finger traces one of the paths. "This is quicker." His digit stops on a large green circle surrounding a blue spot. "But this lake, this we have to cross."

"So?" Shaw says looking between Jeremy and Ellen.

"So," Jeremy answers, "that's a watering hole."

"Which means that any animals in the area would naturally be drawn there and there is nothing on this planet that can disturb a drinking animal and live," Ellen adds.

Shaw nods, impressed, then looks at the map again. "Is that the longer way?"

Jeremy shakes his head. "No. The longer one takes us too close to here." He points to a small building shape. "What we can tell is that it's a bungalow. Once we pass it though, smooth sailing."

Lloyd has that look of someone wanting to ask a question but is afraid to look like an idiot. The others notice but refuse to engage, leaving Ellen to be the one. "What?"

The young man swallows air before speaking. "Well...It's just that...Nobody's told me what the target is?"

Christopher laughs. "That's above your paygrade."

"Wait!" Shaw says. "We're getting paid?"

"That's the thing," Christopher says apologetically. "We are, but..."

Ellen shakes her head as the two men begin squabbling. *Why did I pick 'em?* she thinks before holding up a hand. It instantly works and the two men go quiet. "There," she points at a cleared space on the map that has a small, almost indescribable symbol on it.

Lloyd stares at the map and frowns as he tries to figure out what it means. Then slowly it dawns on him. "It's a generator!"

The woman nods, a sly smile on her face. "That's all we have to do. Blow the power. Easy."

Shaw is shaking his head emphatically as he casually swats at a mosquito. "Won't work. The entire place is powered by geothermal energy; taking out one generator is not going to do anything."

"Glad I'm surrounded by such optimistic lads," Ellen says as she rolls up the map into a tight tube then quickly she tucks it into a metal holder and then checks her watch. "Okay," she says. "Time to move out. No time for lolly-gagging. You gotta pee? Then pee while walking." Without another word she turns and begins trudging through the dense foliage. Jeremy is right behind her.

Lloyd grabs Shaw's arm and asks, "She isn't serious about the peeing?"

Rick Shaw grins. "Welcome to the Alliance."

#

"Well, wasn't that enlightening?" Gideon Pryke says with a loud clap. The sound bounces around the large hall and causes the five men to wince a bit. "Oh, my apologies! Are we suffering a tad?" He laughs then nods to McTiernan. "That'll be all, thank you James."

McTiernan gives a quick curt nod to his boss and the investors before disappearing down the long corridor. Pryke shakes his head with a click of his tongue. "A surly fellow to be sure but he is the best." He casually looks around the main hall of the main resort and makes a mental note about quickly replacing some of the more outdated pieces of art. *Maybe I should commission some of those young upstarts back in Tokyo,* he thinks.

"Wonderful," Winston rumbles. "But what are we waiting for?"

It takes a moment for the owner of Kaiju World to focus on the bulk. He blinks then, "The last guest for the inaugural tour...What? Don't tell me you thought it was just going to be you?" From the sullen looks it's obvious that they did and still do. "Dear fellows," Pryke says. "Originally that was the idea, but the lads in PR thought that a bit of early press--"

"--The press?" Emmerich is fit to burst with rage. The other men stare blankly, trying to figure out why Pryke would invite such a creature.

"That's right," he says with a tone that leaves no room for argument.

"But for the love of God, why?"

Pryke's eyes scan the scared, confused and terrified faces of his investors. The question is quite valid but unfortunately for them, Gideon Pryke has no valid answer of his own other than, "You know what they say? There's no such thing as bad publicity."

Crichton scoffs, even he can't believe it. "Are you fucking joking?"

Pryke shakes his head. Beacham coughs and sputters, "No such thing? No such thing?! Don't you remember what those vultures said about Drummond and Dino Park?"

Tull picks up the refrain, quickly saying, "Yeah! They used the words; deranged megalomaniac, delusional and shyster among the more polite articles."

"Not to mention!" Emmerich adds. "Not to mention that every review for an X-Treme Park has said the exact same thing; you've seen one, you've seen them all. Is that what you want the first written piece to be saying..? Why are you smiling?"

Pryke has a large cheeky grin that seems to say one of two things; just wait and see, or, I'm making this up as I go. For the billionaire owner, both are valid answers. His eyes shift slightly, focusing on the long-legged woman striding towards the group and the smile grows bigger. "Gentlemen, allow me to introduce Teresa Hernandez."

The woman is decked out in jeans and a multi-pocket shirt that is baggy enough to hide her shape. Teresa goes over and shakes Pryke's hand firmly then she looks at the men with pursed lips. "So," she says after a moment of thought. "These are the ones I'm touring with?" There is the slightest hint of an accent but it is her tone of voice that annoys the five men.

Emmerich looks her up and down then says with a chuckle, "Aren't Latinas supposed to be gorgeous and curvy?"

Teresa laughs, "Wow look at that, a Nazi being racist." Her eyes bore into his as she speaks, "Tell ya what Hans, I'll not bother you and you keep your eyes on all the wondrous sights and not me. Oh, and I'll not mention the war."

"I like her!" Winston roars with laughter as they start towards the large doors.

"So, for the tour!" Pryke says as he speeds up to the door. "We'll be visiting the major attractions. As we get to the more...extreme ones we'll have to swap vehicles. Safety at all times."

"We're not going to see that...big motherfucker again?" Tull says nervously.

"Not until Miss Mako gives it the all clear," Pryke says. "It is our first Category 5 and we don't want anything happening to him."

Up till now Teresa has been busy scribbling notes but at the mention of 'Category 5' she looks up at Pryke, "What's a 'Category 5'?"

Gideon Pryke stands in front of the large doors. "Well Miss Hernandez. Our attractions are all rated based on the fabled Serizawa Rating System. Basically it takes the Kaijus and puts them into one of five categories." The doors slowly open silently letting in warm sunlight and a light breeze. "Professor Serizawa, who unfortunately has passed on, came up with the ratings after the Tokyo Attack...It's very easy to understand really." He talks like a teacher explaining simple calculus to a Golden Retriever. "The weakest ones are put in the lowest category, One. Then as they get more powerful and how much damage they can do, we raise their Category with five being the most powerful force in all of creation."

"Umm," Teresa interrupts. "How do you manage the damage?"

"Excellent question! We compare the damage they can do to that of a nuclear bomb." That statement leaves everyone in awe.

With a spin, Pryke pushes the doors open fully and steps out into the bright sun. He races down the steps to the large ATV waiting for them. It has the Kaiju World logo on the sides and the top has been removed and replaced with a clear heavy duty Perspex dome. Pryke stands proudly in front of it and gestures grandly. "Our mode of transportation! Impressive, no?"

The five men look unconvinced as they slowly walk down the steps. Beacham mutters to Tull, "Thought we'd be in tanks or at least a monorail."

Tull nods his agreement and says, "With those beasts roaming about wouldn't it make sense to be in helicopters? Something safer?"

Emmerich slows his own pace and walks next to the two men. He grunts, "Let's see how this goes." His head motions towards the reporter, "If she blasts this place then we can gain total control. Make all the changes we need."

The three men nod and hurry to catch up with the others as Pryke is enthusiastically explaining the vehicle. "The glass is actually a mixture of glass, Perspex and the same material they use on the space shuttles."

"Is NASA still around?" Tull asks.

"Yes," Pryke says, quickly dismissing the quip. "This is the safest land vehicle ever created. It can withstand bullets, missiles and extreme heat."

"And what about nuclear blasts?" Teresa asks without a hint of mockery in her voice. Her tone silences the investors and Pryke gives her a small smile of thanks. She ignores it and repeats the question. "Can it withstand a nuclear attack?"

Gideon Pryke smiles brightly as he opens the doors. "Well, hopefully we'll never have to find out. But all of the technicians and Miss Mako Ikari have all reassured me that it can."

The investors begin to climb up and into the bubble of protection. Only Teresa stands, hands on her hips and a look of scepticism playing on her face. "Not good enough Pryke."

The smile dies slightly on the billionaire's face but he recovers quickly saying, "Let me put it this way, this island is on an underwater volcano which allows us to use the geothermal power. Now, if that volcano was to explode, spewing its red hot lava all over this island, my experts have guaranteed me that this vehicle will survive it. You could drive it all the way to the dock and onto a rescue ship. It's that safe."

Without further word he leaps into the driver's seat then waves for her to follow. With a sigh Teresa Hernandez slowly climbs up and into the converted ATV. "Bully!" Pryke says happily as the vehicle roars to life. Inside the bubble all that they can hear is a soft murmuring from the engines. Pryke gives everyone a thumb up. "It's also sound-proofed. Our boys can get quite rowdy."

"What are we seeing first?" Teresa says as she holds out her cell phone; on the screen is an audio recording program.

"Originally, I thought you'd like to see the Category 1s, but they are for the kids. So, how about we just go for a drive." He doesn't wait for any comments as he pushes the vehicle forwards with a gleeful, "Hi-ho Silver!"

#

Mako Ikari stares at the slumbering monstrosity. The bright blood is seeping through the giant gauze covering the stitches across the base of the thick scaly leathery head. She sighs, amazed that the operation was a success. Anytime something goes right it's considered a success. The woman sighs again then glances at the monitoring program on her tablet. It shows all of the vitals of the Kaiju and so far it reads normal...Except for...

The speakers crackle and Lathrop Preston's voice echoes, "Anything else boss?"

"Why is there a murmur?" Glancing up to the control room, Mako watches the puzzled faces of her team scanning the readings. "It's there," she reaffirms.

"Oh!" Preston's voice is startled. "We don't know...Maybe it's an adverse reaction to the anaesthesia?"

At least he's honest, Mako thinks as she stares at the massive chest cavity that rises and falls with a slight hiccup. She frowns and prays that it's just temporary. Deep down Mako knows that even though it's the first and only Category 5 Kaiju that's been captured, Pryke will have no compunctions destroying the mighty god-like animal. *He's done it before,* she thinks sadly, *what would stop him doing it again?*

"Mako," it's Preston again. "It looks like it's the heart. There's a slight clotting there from the knock-out juice. We're pretty sure that it'll clear out soon enough."

"What if it doesn't?" Once again the resident Kaiju Expert looks up at the control room and watches her team talk rapidly.

When they had first started Pryke's endeavour there was some questioning about how the assets would be conditioned to not follow their natural proclivities. Naturally there had been many ideas bandied about; shock collars, positive reinforcements, and constant drone tracking with missile capabilities. The list went on and on growing more and more ludicrous. Some said that on the island there shouldn't be any need for conditioning, that with hardly any people about and the best security features there would be no need for it. Mako had the perfect idea and she has used it for every single one and so far it had worked.

"Then we'll have a very amazing, still monster," Preston laughs slightly.

Mako frowns and almost shouts, "You're all done! If I need you..." She stops and places a gentle hand on the stirring beast. She shushes at it and slowly the thing goes back to its slumber. "I'm going to stay and try to bond with him," she says softly. "Why don't you all go for a long break," it isn't a request but a hidden order. Her eyes watch the control room slowly begin to empty. The team of people know better than to stay around and watch when she imprints on the creatures.

She sits down, leans against the gigantic jaw and closes her eyes as she begins to hum. This is how it always goes. Slowly the song fills the gigantic room and it echoes eerily. Mako Ikari sings the song that her mother used to sing to her when she had the nightmares. It is haunting and sinuous, that is bitter and sweet all at once, that begins in hello and ends in goodbye. Only a few other living humans have heard it and even then they say nothing, except cry.

As she continues to sing and hum, the massive eyes slowly open and with a wheezing breath Ishiro shifts its head, nudging Mako slightly. To a gigantic creature a nudge is nothing, but to a tiny insignificant human it sends the woman tumbling across the floor.

There is a growl from Ishiro that sounds like an approaching hurricane as it begins to move and try to get to its feet. As the neck bends, it screeches and slams back into the floor, shaking the building, the pain from the operation finally hitting.

Mako is up and trying to run over to the thrashing beast but the hit has rattled her. Her eyes slowly focus on the monster before her and she curses in Japanese. If it continues, she figures, there is a not so slim chance that just from its size and weight, not to mention the strength, Ishiro could destroy the Containment Facility, bringing the land above crashing down and burying everyone. Mako isn't even bothering about the radioactive view and the other powers contained within the mighty terrifying beast.

Her voice carries over the screeching as the tail and talons scratch the floor and walls. The song sounds weaker than before, a tumble will do that, but Mako forces herself to sing loud and clearly. From what she and her team have been able to find out, the Kaijus are not accustomed to music of any kind. In their initial experiments, opera, classical, jazz and easy listening were all tried but each time at the exact moment the song would begin the beast would flip out. Going berserk, destroying valuable equipment and once killing a man. It was by accident that Mako was singing her song and a Category 3 heard it. All were amazed at how quickly the monster had calmed. "Music calms the savage beast," Pryke remarked when told and for some reason he was not surprised.

Slowly Mako walks towards the raging behemoth. Each step she takes gives her voice more power and the Professor can tell that Ishiro is calming. His powerful claws begin to relax, muscles uncoiling as the sound and melody washes over the auditory part of the brain. Its head lowers and a deep wind sounding sigh fills the cavernous room.

Good boy, Mako thinks as she gets close enough to feel the heat radiating from the literal larger than life creature.

Even though the Kaiju's head is flat against the floor, much as a lying dog does, the four large eyes are wide open and they follow Mako's every movement.

She looks down, checking her body and fights the urge to scream. Mako Ikari's skeleton is once again visible. Her clothes, skin, muscles, nerves and organs seem to be phasing. Shifting in and out of view. Part of her knew it was going to happen, but it is still quite a disturbing sight.

How much radiation is bombarding us? Mako answers her own question easily as the room begins to spin and tilt, like some perverted theme park ride. Mako feels the ground rushing to meet her but the leathery hide catches her.

As Mako passes out she hears the same unholy laughter-sound coming from the Category 5 Kaiju.

#

"This is crazy," Teresa says excitedly as she hurriedly scribbles in her notebook. "Amazing, but crazy." She still can't believe what has been shown; these things belong on the silver screen, in the pages of comics or in video games. The first Kaiju that wandered past them without a glance made her scream and almost pee herself. The size and strange looking creature reminded her of something from Stephen King or HP Lovecraft and when she asked everyone what they thought, it annoyed her that the six men were so blasé about it.

Pryke nods humbly as the ATV thunders along the nearly finished road. "We aim to please," he says turning the wheel slightly to avoid a tanker ship sized foot crashing down on the trees. "Hi, Isayama." The foot and leg are covered in quills and the claws retract as the leg moves up and over them. In the imprint left are the quills, each one looks more like a spear than something from a porcupine.

Teresa stares up at the passing monster and her mouth gapes open. "How...?"

"Considering how the Kaijus seem to ignore anything that isn't food, a threat or another Kaiju we aren't worried about them attacking any of the guests," Pryke says, answering her unasked question.

"That's good to know," Teresa says writing down the quote. "But that's not what I was going to ask."

Pryke grunts as the investors chuckle in the back. His eyes dart from the rear-view mirror to the road as he says, "Oh, well what were you going to ask?"

"Where do they come from?"

"He already answered that," Tull says with the same importance of a child.

Ignoring the businessman Teresa asks again, "Where do they come from?"

There is something in her tone that makes Pryke slow the vehicle slightly. He puts it in park then turns to look at her. "Why is that so important?"

Teresa Hernandez blinks then stares at the man. Her words are measured and thought out, "People need to know three things. Where they come from? What is their purpose here?" She looks away, staring at the greenery and serenity around them. "Do they have any rights?"

The last question throws Gideon Pryke for a loop. "Do they have rights? What does that even mean?"

Emmerich groans in the back and stares at the clear roof, there are scratches and other marks of damage. "Hope those are recent," he says, then goes back to paying attention to the two people up front.

"...have rights?" Pryke is asking the woman. "Let me say that again, is there any animal on this planet that has a right? Apart from humans that is."

"All living animals have a right to be free, to be treated with dignity and respect. Are the Kaijus any different?" she says without missing a beat.

A small chuckle is Pryke's answer. He turns back to the road and starts the ATV again, getting it back on the road and pushing it to the max speed as he says, "Here's the thing Teresa. Unlike other animals a Kaiju is capable of doing something the others cannot. Mainly, destroying a city and killing millions. That means they are a threat, and a threat has no rights." With all the bumps the speeding ATV feels like a rickety old roller coaster. "By bringing them here," Pryke continues, "we are guaranteeing that these wondrous creatures have the right to live, for if they were to stay put near whichever city they pop up, they surely would be killed."

The group is silent as Teresa writes everything that Pryke just said. Her lips are pursed and there is a cute crease in her brow. They hit a bump and she drops her pen with a curse. Fumbling, she finally grabs it then continues her questioning, "So, what you're saying is that because you're protecting them, that gives you the right to do whatever you want to these animals?"

Beacham mutters to no-one in particular, "Great, a discussion on ethics."

"Hope it's not always like this," Tull agrees.

Pryke licks his lips. "To answer your question with just one word...Yes."

The stunned silence is oppressive as not one person has any idea how to respond to the amount of hubris coming from the owner of the island. Teresa taps the pen on her leg and notices a sign that reads: GLADIATORIAL FIELDS. The pen stops tapping. "Where are you taking us?"

"Just to one of the most entertaining places on the island," Pryke says as the vehicle crests a ridge. "See, it doesn't matter whether or not people enjoy the experience of seeing these magnificent creatures roaming freely. What they really want to see is the fighting."

Before them is a perfect replica of the Roman Coliseum, only twenty times the size. "To accommodate the Kaiju and the audience," Pryke says as they get closer. There are sections that are still being welded into place. "Sure, there are still things to be added. But just imagine, the roar of the crowd as two or more of the monsters do deadly battle for our pleasure." As he stops the vehicle, they see another sign welcoming guests to: KAIJU GAMES, CAUTION THERE MAY BE GRAPHIC DEPICTIONS OF VIOLENCE.

"We're gonna make billions," Winston says with a hungry growl.

CHAPTER SEVEN

"What the fuck is that?" Lloyd Behm screams as the giant demon from hell roars again.

The attack came without warning. One moment the forest is peaceful and just lovely, then the massive claws came thundering down and the four horned beast screamed at the stunned members of Animal Alliance. They had no idea what they would encounter on the island, but for sure none of them had expected to see what they can only describe as something from a nightmare; four long horns protruding from the face, two from the brow and two from the jaws. When the beast roars, a wave of heat burns the leaves and singes the clothing of the people.

"What. The. Fuck. Is. That?" Lloyd asks again, this time slightly calmer.

Ellen smiles at the sight. "That's what we're here to--"

Her voice is cut off as the Kaiju's tail whips over their heads; the whooshing of the air whips the hair of each person around. They all duck down as the long, whip like tri-pronged tail slams into the ground, trying to impale the tiny screaming humans. Rolling and dodging away, each one trying not to be staked while Lloyd pulls out his weapon and opens fire, squeezing the trigger as he screams in terror, the tiny chunks of lead bouncing off of the thick skin.

"Lloyd!" Ellen shouts as the others slowly back away making a hasty retreat. "Stop wasting ammo!"

But the new recruit can't hear her over the pounding of his blood racing through his veins and the adrenaline controlling his movements. "Die hellspawn!" he hollers at the monster, who seems to be having a blast playing with something new. Of course it is a subjective term since a cat playing with a mouse is horrific to the mouse, much in the same way a child pulling wings off flies is. The Kaiju's tail moves faster than a cobra which is surprising considering its size.

Each time the tail misses its target a cloud of dirt and debris is kicked up and craters are left in the jungle floor. The trees shake and some topple, crashing into one another.

"Lloyd!" Ellen screams again, her voice sounding distant to herself, tugging on the man's arm. "We've got to go! Now!"

The monster raises its tail high into the air and there is a moment of serenity as Lloyd Behm glances at Ellen and says, "Go--"

His voice gurgles as dark red blood froths and then drips from the corners of his mouth. The young man shudders as he stares uncomprehending at Ellen. One of his hands touches his chest causing him to whimper.

Ellen Scott stumbles back as the dying man is lifted up off the ground. The centre prong of the tail sticking out of his stomach, blood and acidic juices drip from the tip. Lloyd groans then screams as the tail whips him about. The sheer force of each rapid movement liquefying bones. His screams snap Ellen out of her shock and the woman runs. Not daring to look back until she feels safe enough.

She doesn't get far as one of the gigantic clawed feet slams into the ground before her. The impact sends out a shockwave that forces the woman to the ground. She flattens herself, trying to cover as much ground as possible, just in case cracks form, then looks around frantically trying to find the rest of her team. The roar grabs her attention and she turns to see the horror befalling Lloyd.

The limp body dangles in the wind, limbs now nothing but loose wet pieces of flesh. She can't make out if he is dead because of the distance but also Lloyd's head is hanging limply against his chest. *Why the fuck didn't you run?* She thinks, wishing to know what the man was thinking. But deep down she knows that his fate is sealed.

"Fuck, fuck, fuck, fuckety, fuck!" Rick Shaw's voice makes her squeak. The man's under a fallen tree, safe from the catastrophe happening around them. Ellen can see that lying next to him, curled up in a ball is Christopher and Jeremy who are staring in awe.

"Shaw!" Ellen whispers loudly, doing everything she can not to draw any attention.

Jeremy's eyes shift and he notices her, "Gods!"

Fuck, they're gone!

"Look!" Shaw shouts.

All eyes, including Christopher's go to the ghastly sight; the Kaiju is staring at the small body, almost like it is studying the tiny human. It shakes its tail which gets a tiny groan of pain. The beast growls then flicks the end of its tail with a surprising dexterity. The force pushes Lloyd's body off it and into the air. The tiny human spins and tumbles like a rag doll. The body's path is heading straight for the gaping maw of the monster.

As Lloyd's limp body just passes the threshold of the large spiky teeth, the powerful jaws clamp shut trapping the man. Lloyd screams as blood erupts in a fountain from his torso.

"We've got to go," Ellen hisses, her voice startling the three men. They turn to her, looking for leadership. "What's the best way?"

Jeremy doesn't say anything as he points dumbly. Ellen can't believe it, he wants them to run under the belly of the--

"No," Shaw mutters.

They can see what he is talking about. Lloyd's face and arms are swelling. Puffing up from the pressure being forced into them, his blood and other bodily fluids fighting to break free and any minute now...

Ellen, Shaw, Christopher and Jeremy don't hear the pop. Instead they see Lloyd Behm explode, his skin tearing then disintegrating in a vaporous cloud. The Kaiju happily begins chewing on the flaps of skin and other remains and it seems to be purring contentedly.

"Now!"

The order spurs the men, who get to their feet wobbly and run. Following Ellen Scott who is doing everything in her power to push away the image of the exploding man. *Move your ass,* she repeats to herself over and over.

Each man catches up to her and they all run in silence letting Jeremy lead the way while they all try to forget the sight. But each knows deep in their heart of hearts that it will never happen.

#

"Ah excellent!" Gideon Pryke exclaims happily as the wait-staff finish serving the delicious food. "Chef has really outdone himself. Really he has."

Before Pryke, Teresa Hernandez and the five investors is a plethora of culinary delights; fresh sushi, smoked salmon, a variety of chicken dishes, dim-sums, spring rolls and what could only be described as duck burgers. Being served along with the smorgasbord of food is a bevy of the finest alcoholic beverages; whisky, tequila, rum, wine (both red and white) and beers.

Pryke looks at the guests who are all staring at the food with a mixed look of hunger and disgust. "That's always the reaction first time at the arena," he says with a wave of his hand as she sits. "You'll get over it quickly. Think of it like watching Discovery Channel." He sniffs the food then smiles eagerly, "Wonderful!"

One by one the men begin to sit and pick up the steins filled with fine ales. Only Teresa stands, her face ashen grey and her eyes burning with passion. Pryke notices this and sighs, "What is it Teresa? Another ethical dilemma?"

Slowly the reporter nods. "You can call it ethical or moral. What I call it is cruelty to animals, barbaric and savage!" Her raised voice stops the six men who all turn to stare at her. "Are you out of your mind?" the woman continues hotly. "How dare you force these animals to fight!"

Gideon Pryke motions with his hands for the investors to continue eating and drinking. As they do he locks eyes with Teresa and takes a moment before speaking, "Who said I was forcing them to do anything?"

His calmness fans her fury even more. "Out there is a coliseum! Why else would you have it?"

"A tribute to the Romans."

"Mister Pryke, do not patronize me," her tone is deadly serious.

The owner of Kaiju World slowly gets to his feet and begins to walk the length of the table towards Teresa. "Miss Hernandez," he begins with a similar tone to hers. "You seem to misunderstand what I'm doing. The island, the park, the Kaijus are all for one reason. To educate. Right now, at this very moment, all over the world people, scientists and governments are scared of these 'devils'. Kaiju World's aim is to teach the planet that they are nothing but innocent animals surrounded by the worst monsters on the entire planet. Humans."

Teresa chuckles and shakes her head, "You sound just like Sean Drummond."

A champagne flute shatters against the wall as Pryke snarls, "Don't you dare compare me to that charlatan! What he did was create a cash-cow that bit his own hand. I've taken my time, hired the best of the best and I am not taking anything for granted."

Teresa smiles. "If this is a place of education, then why have the arena?"

The man blinks as he realises that she has him trapped. This makes him laugh. "Why else? To give the people what they want...Please, sit." As the reporter glides into her chair Pryke goes back to his own seat. "Think about the King of Monster movies. What were the highest grossing ones? The ones that are always talked about by the fans?" He is expecting the blank faces from the gathered people and Pryke smiles. "The battles against other monsters! 'All Monsters Attack', 'Godzilla vs King Kong' and 'Destroy All Monsters'...hell, any time Godzilla fought another monster the public came out in droves...Look, what I'm saying is that the paying public love to watch titans do glorious battle. And if they are paying to come to this place and seeing real monsters, up close and personal, why shouldn't they get to see them fight?"

"Because it isn't right!" Teresa says sounding exasperated. "Do you enjoy the bull fights in Spain? Or how about the way the Japanese make their food from sea-animals while the poor things are still living?" She continues talking, cutting off the philanthropist, "Would you agree, Mister Pryke, that just because we have sentience, the ability to experience existential terror we have dominion over the planet? That we have the right to treat animals of any kind, however we want to?"

"Well, no, not exactly," Pryke is forced to admit.

"Then!" the woman says victoriously. "Why have them fight? Isn't it the same thing? The bull fights, seafood restaurants, our own fears? Aren't you being hypocritical?"

"No," a small voice says from behind Teresa. Spinning, the reporter is startled to see Mako Ikari. She bows to the men as she walks over to the table. "Forgive my lateness."

"Think nothing of it," Pryke says as he helps Mako into her seat.

"Who is this?"

"Mako Ikari," Mako says. "I'm the head of Kaiju Research."

Teresa nods suspiciously even though she is happy to have another woman in the room, "So, why do you say 'no'?"

Mako swallows the piece of sushi she is chewing on and has a sip of beer. "These are not animals as we think of the term. The definition of an animal is; any living thing other than a human. The Kaijus have trace amounts of DNA that we can find in humans. This means that they are related to us on some distant level."

"So? Can't we trace all life to the same beginning?"

The professor nods. "True, but, the thing about these creatures, which is a better definition, is that we don't know where they come from."

"What?" Teresa scoffs.

Mako nods and looks to Pryke who says, "That is the sad truth of the matter."

"Which is why you can't say that they have the same rights as any other animal?" Teresa asks sceptically.

"In a word, yes. But it comes down to something more important than your own ideas of ethics and morals," Mako says. "These beings have a natural need to fight and destroy. In the same exact way that us humans have that natural need."

She sips from the beer again before continuing, "The Romans had the games in the Coliseum which leads us to sports. First there was wrestling which was the tamed version of the gladiatorial battles. After that we had boxing which is more of the same."

Mako looks at the entire table and smiles slightly. "Take that away from us and what happens? Reality TV. They are the same, without this outlet of energy and aggression they become depressed and eventually die," she glances to Pryke quickly. "This is the reason for the arena. So they can do what it is they have always done, destroy and fight."

"Let them fight," Crichton says eliciting a small chuckle from his partners.

"You laugh," Mako says sternly. "But the truth is that it would be crueller not to let them fight."

#

"What is it doing?" James McTiernan asks no-one in particular as he stares at the monitor.

On the screen the Kaiju's tail swishes back and forth, in a steady rhythm that is almost hypnotic. While the tail sways and bounces, the front legs tap on the floor in a gentle beating as if playing the bongos. But the thing that has gotten the entirety of Security on edge is the enormous, scarred ferocious face. Ishiro's eyes seem to be staring at the multitudes of cameras and every time McTiernan moves slightly, the eyes shift, seemingly following his every move.

"That's not right," Chris Winder says softly and he sighs when he hears the various agreeable grunts. Nearly all the men and women who work in the security department have been trained, whether subliminal or standardized, to withstand anything that can be considered out of the ordinary or F.U.B.A.R. Which, considering the gigantic city destroying monster currently staring at them through the monitors is pushing their training to the limits.

JR Handley shakes his head and quickly turns away, "I didn't sign up for this."

"Then what did you sign up for?" Donna Mixon barks at him from across the room. "You wanna go back to the firing line?"

Handley shakes his head as he mutters, "Not really, but it might be better than having to stare at that thing all day."

"Turn it off," McTiernan says tiredly. "Save us having to hear you bitch and moan about it." That gets a slight chuckle and the Head of Kaiju World Security glances at his tablet. It has various alerts flashing on the screen. "Anyone know where A.R. Team is currently?"

Simpson raises his hand. "Sir, they haven't set out yet."

"Damn it," McTiernan says clenching his hands. "Show me satellite."

The main screen flashes from the grinning Ishiro to a high-quality live streaming image of the island. The topography isn't hard to decipher and after years of staring at it McTiernan is an expert at reading the layout. "Zoom in on the LZ," he says with a sigh. *Should've sent out my own boys,* he thinks as the satellite image becomes pixelated each time the camera zooms in.

"Google Maps would be faster," Nathan Pedde says without a trace of sarcasm.

"Stow it," McTiernan orders even though he agrees. *Fucking S&P,* he thinks, *as useless as tits on a bull.*

As the image clears, everyone in the room can clearly see the small outline of the boat. James McTiernan swears and tosses the tablet to the tiled floor where it cracks. "Where the fuck are they?!" he barks as his eyes scan the faces of his team. "How could that," he points to the main screen, "how could that happen?"

"Sir," Donna says not afraid of their CO. "You might want to see this." She isn't asking or advising. Not Donna.

"Fine," McTiernan says with a wave of his hand.

Once more the screen flashes and the room gasps. These men and women have seen violence like no other; Afghanistan, Burma, Mexico and South Africa. They've witnessed killing fields littered with the dead, lynching of entire families, disembowelled bodies left on the streets as warnings, dog fights, children used for target practice and every conceivable way to hurt, maim and kill a human. But nothing has prepared them for this sight.

Bright orange fluorescent blood covers the walls, ceiling, floor and any other surface of the holding pen. "Looks like a Pollack," Donna mutters but even she is taken aback by how quickly the blood splattering happened.

"What the...Zoom in on that thing!" McTiernan's order is rapidly carried out and the entire Security Team can see the cause. Most wish they had not.

Ishiro smiles at the cameras, its four eyes unmoving and unblinking. From the enormous mouth hangs tatters and shreds of dark leathery flesh. Slowly and deliberately the monsters raises a leg and waves a bloodied stump. From where the foot used to be McTiernan and his team can just make out the tip of a shard of bone protruding from the bloody pulp.

"Did it do that to itself?" Simpson asks quietly.

McTiernan begins to open his mouth then forgets what he was

going to say. The Category 5 Kaiju begins to chew on its own flesh and bones, the large horrid tongue slurping and flicking up the meat so the gigantic fangs can further tear up the meal. What makes the sight seem truly unnerving is the way the eyes never seem to move. They stare defiantly into the cameras, as if saying "Whatcha gonna do now?"

"I want that thing sedated and the room completely sealed off from everyone," McTiernan says. He glances at his people who are still in shock. "Move it!" His commanding voice pushes the team into action. The CO watches the screen and smiles slightly as the small tranquilizer darts fire rapidly, embedding into the thick skin and injecting the sedative. "Don't stop until that thing is down."

He looks to Winder and Handley, "Send another message to A.R. Team. Get their asses moving." McTiernan doesn't bother waiting for a reply as he looks back to the main screen. "Send a screenshot to Ikari. She'll want to see this."

"Already done," Donna says.

James McTiernan nods his thanks as he thinks, *What else can go wrong?* The moment they had gotten word of Ishiro's appearance in Acapulco he had been the only one to protest the idea, the only one to remind Pryke about Dino Park and how it had been the lack of control that had caused its downfall. Gideon Pryke had laughed it off and soothed him with just one small sentence, "That's why I have you. Control."

How can I control a God? McTiernan now thinks as his mind begins pondering all of the worst case scenarios. Each one bloodier and more terrible than the last.

#

"That's a God!" Jeremy Smith exults the moment he finishes catching his breath.

None of the members of Animal Alliance know how long they ran for, nor how far. The only things that they are one-hundred percent positive about are that Lloyd Behm is dead and that a creature from their worst nightmares ate him. It was only when they couldn't hear the thundering crashing of massive feet or the earth-cracking roar that the four people collapsed. Their lungs and muscles burning after the extreme effort. And it is Jeremy who speaks first.

"That was a God!" he repeats, his voice filled with shock and awe.

Christopher Michael scoffs and shakes his head. "You dolt! Why would a God eat Lloyd?"

Jeremy scratches his head as he thinks. It is a good question, he must admit, but there is a reason for everything.

"While he thinks," Christopher says looking at Rick Shaw and Ellen. "What's the game-plan? We turning back and getting the flying fuck out of here?"

Ellen Scott looks frazzled; her expression is one of disbelief and abject terror. "I thought they were joking," she whispers.

"Boss," Shaw says gently shaking her arm. "You okay?"

"Divinity affects us all in different ways," intones Jeremy. His eyes are wide and filled with joy. "Poor Lloyd could not handle the stress of being so close to a God."

Christopher's face clouds over and he snarls, "That's not a God. It's a monster!"

A monster not a God, Ellen blinks as the thought hits her mind. For the briefest moment she felt as if the universe had opened and she knew that humanity was insignificant, but Christopher's words brought reality back to her. "And that is the reason we're here," she says, her voice sounding less shaky and her eyes now looking clearer. The woman wipes sweat from her face, "Some say they--"

"--They!" Shaw says frantically. "There's more than one?!"

"There's always more than one and we should all endeavour to be loyal servants."

"Pipe down," Christopher hushes Jeremy before turning to Ellen. "What did we actually sign up for?"

"Protect and help all living creatures from the evils of men," Jeremy says. He cries out and grabs his nose, trying to stave the blood flowing from his nostrils.

"Feel better?" Shaw asks with a slight grin.

Christopher nods then winces, holding his hand and checking his knuckles. "Damn! That hurts."

"You sucker punched me!"

"Well, I did tell you to keep ya trap shut."

The two men stare at each other, both sizing the other up, ready for a fight. But neither is ready to throw the first punch. Robert Shaw and Ellen Scott watch and wait.

"You're not worth my time," Jeremy says after a tense minute. "My God will smite you."

"Oh," Christopher says. "He'll smite me! Oh please don't let the God get me--"

He cries out as the ground smacks the back of his head hard. Jeremy and Christopher roll through the underbrush; fists flying, arms flailing and legs kicking up dirt and dust. Every third hit lands with wet sounding slaps. The fight looks more like a tussle or lovers embracing.

"How come real fights never look as good as movie ones?"

Ellen shrugs, "Maybe because nobody wants reality."

Shaw nods. "So what is the plan..? Tell me you have a plan?"

The woman smiles slyly. "Don't I always?"

Before Shaw can answer, the woman gets to her feet and is quickly over at the tussling men. Two rapid kicks later and the men groan and roll apart, holding their groins. Ellen looks down at them. "Done?"

Jeremy nods through the pain while Christopher tries not to vomit from the kick.

"We need to get a fix on our position. From there we can get back on track and finish this," Ellen says with a nod.

"So," Shaw slowly says, drawing out the word. "We're still on?"

"Naturally. I've never failed a mission and don't intend to start now." The three men watch as their leader crouches down in front of them. "What attacked us is a Kaiju or a monster if that's easier to swallow. This island is littered with them. We're here to make sure that none are used by humans. Specifically two; Gideon Pryke and Mako Ikari."

"Fuck me," Christopher sighs. "It's another Dino Park."

"More or less," Ellen says after a slight pause. "The only difference is that here the animals have the ability to destroy a city. But," she holds up a hand, silencing the men, "it doesn't mean we give up. We must finish the job."

Shaw looks sceptical as he speaks, "That's all well and good. But what's the plan? We blow up the generator and then what? Saunter back to the boat?" He laughs. "Correct me if I'm wrong, but once the power's gone won't all hell break loose?"

"Yes," Ellen says her voice full of confidence. "All we have to do is mingle with the workers and be evaced with them. Piece of cake."

"All while not getting eaten or stomped," Christopher snarks.

"There are worst things," Jeremy says as he sits up. "These are gods and when they get a taste of freedom nothing will curb their vengeance."

The smile Ellen Scott gives the men chills every single one of them. "I'm counting on it."

CHAPTER EIGHT

"I'm not going to bore you with the attractions for the kids," Pryke says as the Tour ATV roars across a bridge.

Lunch had ended quickly the moment Mako Ikari received the message. She hurriedly excused herself and ran from the room leaving the confused people to be guided back to the long protective vehicle. Gideon Pryke chatted happily as they passed through gates and next to fences.

"What are the fences for?" Crichton asks from the back.

"To stop the Kaiju wandering freely," snarks Teresa.

Pryke chuckles, "Not exactly Teresa." He is behaving like they didn't argue earlier. "All of the fences are in place to make sure that our guests don't go off and get in trouble."

"Who'd be stupid enough to go looking for a city destroying monster?" Emmerich snorts.

Another chuckle from the owner. "You'd be surprised. Very surprised." He slows the vehicle slightly as they come to a thick clump of trees. "So far, lady and gents, you have all seen the more family friendly aspects of the park."

"Yeah, including a cage fight ring," Teresa says again. Everyone in the car knows that both Pryke and Mako are right in having the arena. Professor Ikari made that abundantly clear. So to the investors it is silly that the reporter is acting a child.

"Nothing so mundane," Pryke says as the vehicle enters the small forest. He flicks on the six lights adorning the front.

"Are we in a Mizayaki movie?" Beacham says.

"As long as it isn't a Paul Cooley book," Tull replies. This gets a chuckle from the other investors.

"Could be worse," Winston rumbles. "Could be a Michael Bay movie."

They laugh loudly at that except for Emmerich who looks hurt. "I like Bay," he says sullenly.

"You also like Sharknado," Tull roars with laughter.

"No accounting for taste," Teresa says expertly ending the frivolity. "Where are we going?"

"To what Publicity says is going to be the most popular experience Kaiju World has to offer. This is really the chance of a lifetime. Adventure like no other," Pryke pauses to focus on turning the wheel. "The extreme sports fans are going to love it."

"Just spit it out man!" Winston growls.

Gideon Pryke laughs, "What is the best part of Neon Genesis, Gundam and Pacific Rim?"

The question hangs in the air as the ATV nears the exit. A bright light grows bigger the closer they get to the exit. "Anyone? No?" Pryke is genuinely surprised at the blank stares. He shrugs. "The best part of those is what humanity uses to fight."

"No fucking way!" Tull says excitedly. He's figured out where they are going.

Pryke nods and winks at Teresa before saying, "Yes fucking way. Gentlemen...and dear lady. Welcome to our Mech-Yard!" The vehicle bursts from the tunnel of trees into the sunlight. Even with the dark storm clouds forming they have to blink before their eyes adjust to the rays. When each one is able to see clearly again the men and woman gasp and marvel at the structure towering over the vehicle and land; it looks the same as an ancient temple from Mesoamerica, stone steps and cement forms each level of the impressive construct. It looks old, aged and cracks spider-web across the rocks and moss grows strategically on the corners and in the cracks.

"Is that Mexican?" Teresa asks with a confused tone.

Below the pyramid a large electric-fence surrounded ring is visible. Like all other fences on Maikeru Island they are reinforced with steel beams and each wire is as thick as a man. At each of the four corners stand towers with security bunkers atop each one, they are fully automated. Each one has a huge rail-gun that throws the view slightly askew.

"Mexican?" Pryke is confused. "Why would we have anything from the Americas?"

"The Aztec Temple."

Gideon Pryke laughs as he brings the vehicle to a stop. He looks at the six people. "On top of the temple, which is not from any particular place," he winks again at Teresa. "At the top is the greatest treasure known to mankind. Whenever the moon is red a challenger will be brought forth to battle for the treasure. If that challenger can beat the champion in three rounds then the treasure shall be theirs." He opens the door and the others follow suit. With the cloud covering the sun the area is much cooler and the ring seems much more ominous.

"What's the prize?" Emmerich asks, his eyes big and hungry.

Pryke shrugs. "Could be money, a free stay at Kaiju World or something amazing...Just think of it as fortune and glory. Would you believe this is my favourite thing to do when I'm feeling stressed."

The group begins walking and their eyes go to the armed towers. The armaments track them, the barrels following every single step each person takes.

"Anyone else not comfortable with those?" Crichton says.

"Don't worry m'boy," Pryke says offhandedly. "They only fire on the Kaijus. They are programmed to track and attack their DNA."

Beacham says, "So the Kaijus are needed for this too?" It isn't so much a statement and the man waits for an answer.

"Obviously," Teresa beats Pryke to the punch. "What were you expecting? A T-Rex." This gets a good laugh from the others and Teresa glares at each man. "I'm not being funny," she snaps before pointing. "What's in there?"

They follow her arm and see the large dark building. It stands at least four-hundred meters high and is clearly a hangar. Pryke stands in front of it and holds his arms out wide, "Lady and Gentlemen! Boys and girls of all ages! Welcome to the very best--"

"--Get on with it!" Winston rumbles deeply.

The wind promptly taken out of Pryke's sails, the man tries to hide his pout of disappointment by turning to the doors. "Here is the crowning achievement of Kaiju World!" He presses a button on a remote and sirens blare, screaming to life as the heavy doors begin to screech open. "Mechs Versus Kaijus," Pryke says as three giant human-shaped robots are slowly illuminated.

#

"How much farther?" Rick Shaw whines again for the tenth time in the past hour.

Jeremy stops hiking and slowly turns. His face is covered in sweat and his long dark thick hair is matted to his neck and brow. With the circles under his eyes the man looks quite crazy and totally don't-fuck-with-me.

"Well?" Christopher asks ignoring the death stare he is receiving.

"Keep your mouth shut," Jeremy says while tapping a finger on Shaw's chest.

"Why?" the man says all bluster. "You wanna go again?"

It's Rick Shaw who steps between the two men quickly, saying, "You know what guys? How about we get a beer and watch some tits fly, huh? Then after that how about we go for wings and then catch a movie? Sounds good, yeah?"

"The fuck you talking about?" Christopher glances at Jeremy who shares the confused look.

"Or, how about some horse racing? A bit of gambling, yeah?" Shaw continues.

Jeremy turns to Ellen, "Is he okay?"

"That's exactly how you two idiots sound everytime one of you opens your cock-sucking mouth," Shaw says, slapping both men up the sides of their heads. "Get the fuck back in the game...okay? Do you wanna end up like Lloyd? Because the way you two keep screaming and carrying on, there is bound to be another attack and I for one do not want to be goddamn Kaiju shit anytime soon...So calm the fuck down!" Without another word he starts off again stalking into the lush forest of the island.

Ellen follows him and says softly as she passes the two men, "Keep your periods from syncing up, okay."

"So, how far to go?" Christopher asks again with an outstretched hand as an apology.

Jeremy shakes the hand as he quickly looks around. "Hang on." Without warning he scampers up a tall tree, easily finding foot and hand-holds. He grips a vine and hangs slightly forward, his heavy body causing the vine to groan and stretch. "Not far," he calls down with a big grin. "Another hundred meters or so."

"Then get your ass in gear!" Ellen calls to the two stragglers.

"Yes Ma'am!" Christopher salutes with a chuckle as he takes off at a jog, leaving Jeremy alone.

The tall man lands on the ground in a crouch and grunts. He looks at his right hand; fresh blood covers his palm and drips down onto the dirt. Slowly Jeremy finds the rough end of the shard of bark and yanks it out. The moment it is free more dark blood flows. He has to cup his hand to keep it from overflowing.

"This is for you, my Gods," he whispers while wiping the bloodied hand onto the trunk of a tree. He looks at the odd angular symbol he has painted and whispers again, "When your judgment is upon this world, remember my sacrifices."

"Jeremy, nut up or shut up!"

The call makes the man blink. Looking around he takes off at a gallop, his long legs allowing him to catch-up quickly with the group.

"You okay?" Ellen asks as they all fall into a matching pace.

"Yep, needed a better view to place us."

"And?"

He gestures, "About fifty meters that way."

Ellen nods and glances at the direction pointed. "Then let's move out."

Christopher goes over to Shaw. "Can't wait for a cool beer."

The other man smiles. "Got a six-pack cooling on the boat."

"Then what are we waiting--"

The roar stops the men cold in their tracks. It's higher in pitch than the previous one they heard. Jeremy smiles slightly as Christopher and Shaw hurry over to Ellen and him, their eyes wide and it's obvious that they are scared.

"Do you think we can make it?" Ellen asks as another roar shakes them.

"Depends on where it is."

"You've got to be fucking kidding me," Shaw says with a big sigh.

"Don't say it," Christopher sighs as well.

Shaw nods and instead of speaking he uses his head to gesture, alerting the others to the heavy breathing behind them. They don't want to turn, not wanting to see the gaping maw filled with gigantic teeth, and none want to be swallowed whole.

"How the fuck did it sneak up on us?" Christopher whispers.

"The roar was probably a distraction," Ellen says.

"What do we do boss?" Shaw whimpers.

"Get to the generator."

"When?"

The deep hurricane breathing stops and the entire jungle goes quiet. All that the four people can hear is their own breathing, the rapid beating of their hearts and the slight crunch of the dried leaves under their feet.

A hundred to one we make it, Ellen calculates the odds of outrunning the monster and the defeatist in her knows that it would take a miracle. "Don't breathe," she whispers.

Loud, hungry, agitated sniffing surrounds the members of Animal Alliance. The Kaiju is trying to track them.

"Its vision must be based on movement," Shaw says with a chuckle.

In response to the laughter the beast roars again. Spittle flies and covers the backs of the people from head to toe with thick saliva. The smell makes the three men and the woman gag and they have to force themselves to not lose their food.

"Go," Ellen says. *If we can make it to the generator maybe the blast will take out this monster.* She realizes what she just thought and for a brief moment Ellen Scott hates herself.

Fucking humanity, she thinks as her legs carry her forward. *Always putting itself before the lives of animals.* Ellen blinks and ducks, dodging a low hanging tree branch.

Quickly she glances to the left and then the right and smiles slightly. Her team is right there, they are in a line; each one doing their best to make it to the generator.

"Is it following us?" Shaw yells.

In answer they hear the thundering footsteps and the crashing of trees behind them.

"Fuckfuckfuckfuckfuckfuckfuckfuck!" Christopher screams as his legs pump harder and harder.

"There!" Jeremy shouts as the Power Generator comes into view; the large squat cement buildings have no wires or transformers running from the roof nor are there any fences, it is as unremarkable as any building ever constructed.

"You sure that's it?" Christopher cries out as he leaps over a fallen tree.

"Doesn't matter," Ellen speeds up. "It goes down which is good for us. Get in there now!"

The thundering of the Kaiju is growing closer which forces the small tiny people to run harder and faster. They are not only racing certain death, but also each other.

The door is unlocked and Ellen slams it shut.

The sudden darkness renders them blind but it doesn't take Shaw long to find the light-switch. As the lights flicker on, the members of Animal Alliance see a long steel and mesh corridor that leads to a staircase going down. Ellen goes over, ignoring her men who are trying to catch their breaths and not pass out, and looks down the staircase. It goes down to a small door. Above is a sign that reads: DANGER POWER GENERATOR & CONTROL.

Ellen smiles and turns back saying, "Jeremy, you stay and keep an eye on that thing outside." Outside they can hear stomping thundering steps as the monster stalks about in frustration. "Shaw and Christopher get yourselves down there and plant the bombs."

Without a word the two men march past her and disappear down the stairs. Ellen looks over at Jeremy and frowns slightly, "How's the hand?"

He grunts and opens the door a crack. An ear-splitting roar fills the room and the man quickly slams the door shut. "Not too smart is it?"

Ellen shakes her head and goes over to him, "So, do you really think they are Gods...or are you just bullshitting?"

The look Jeremy Smith gives Ellen speaks volumes but his words hit her hard. "In a world where the major religions have no definitive proof of the existence of divinity, why wouldn't you get down and worship them?"

"But what about the destruction each one of these things can--"

"--All ready boss," Shaw says with a grin on his face. The man has always loved blowing shit up.

"Okay," Christopher hands Ellen the detonator and taps her shoulder. "So, how do we get out of here?"

"Just run," she answers. The looks her men give her are all the same; total disbelief. "I know it's slim," she says. "But that's the best we can do...How big is the blast going to be?"

Both Shaw and Christopher quickly look at each other, then to their leader and they shrug. "No idea boss," Shaw says.

"Yeah," Christopher joins in. "Could just take out the building, but looking at the setup there it could go bigger. We are using at least twenty pounds of C4."

"Could it take out the Kaiju?" Jeremy sounds genuinely concerned for the safety of the monster that can kill all of them as easily as a cat could a mouse.

"Nah," Shaw shakes his head. "It'd take more than this to do any real damage."

"But there is a chance?"

Shaw sighs and looks to Ellen. "It's your say boss. Either we blow it the moment we get to safety and risk hurting the little tyke...or we run like hell and risk the explosion."

Ellen looks at her watch, *We're running out of time...*"Fuck it," she says after a moment of silence. "We go now and blow it. There are plenty of these things on this island." She looks to Jeremy. "Chances are it'll get burnt a little, but that'll be all. It'll be fine."

Her tone is the same that parents use on children when they are obviously lying to them. But just like every child in the world who accepts it, Jeremy nods after scanning each face of his teammates.

"On the count of three," Ellen says as they line up behind Jeremy. "The moment we hit the tree-line I'm gonna blow it."

The men nod and their muscles tense up. Ellen Scott takes a deep breath and closes her eyes. "One," she counts slowly. "Two," she can feel her own muscles begin to tense as she gets ready to run past the monster. This is their only chance and if it looks like the Kaiju is going to get her then she'll blow the generator. Her hand feels slick and wet squeezing the plastic detonator; it only has two buttons, one for arming and the other to cause the actual explosion. *Is there a range on this thing?* she thinks but pushes the thought away as the adrenaline fills her veins.

"Three!"

CHAPTER NINE

Ten seconds.

That's how long it takes before the emergency lights cast the containment room in an eerie beautiful purple glow. The blue lights mix with the glowing orange blood from Ishiro, the park's only Category 5 Kaiju. Professor Mako Ikari's brow furrows as she silently counts down to when the geothermic power should kick in. *One minute delay*, she reminds herself. Of course with how many problems the island facility is being plagued with, Software & Programming only focuses on the most important matters. In other words; whichever one Gideon Pryke tells them to do first.

The low rumble from the heavily sedated Kaiju has the same timbre as that of a lonely cat's cry. Mako places a gentle hand on the jowl and says softly, "I'm sorry. I am so so sorry but it is for your own good."

When Mako had arrived at the Control Room in Containment and saw the violence and bloodshed for herself, the woman had no idea how to react. She wanted to fire every man and woman on her team who had allowed this to happen. A part of her screams at her to ignore all procedures and run into the massive chamber to check on the beast. The amount of blood and the stump made her want to vomit. Mako is a true bag of mixed emotions.

But as always it is the rational side of her that won. Mako rattled off her commands, biting off each word; Sedate. Clean up. Stop the wound from getting infected. She would go down and see to the Kaiju herself.

Now, standing in the faintly lit room Mako can feel her pulse begin to speed up. She closes her eyes. *It's only darkness,* she tells herself. *The power will come back on. It has to!* The woman doesn't want to think about all the possibilities if it doesn't return. She knows that Gideon Pryke is a little worried that the investors will pull all of the funding for the park. But Mako isn't worried. Her keen mind has already started working on a contingency plan; there are only two people so far who know about it, Mako and Pryke. "You'll do just nicely," she whispers to Ishiro.

She gasps as her phone starts vibrating, pulsing quickly and buzzing loudly. Mako had forgotten that the cell phones use their own satellite, thanks to one of the many divisions Pryke owns. Without another moment's hesitation she pulls her phone out. "What's going on?"

Brad Carsten's voice is a little shaky as he speaks, "There's been an attack!"

"What?" Mako walks away from the sedated behemoth.

"You heard," all formality is gone from the man's voice. "We got the notification just before the power went down."

So it is an outage, Mako thinks. *But why hasn't the backup kicked in?*

"Boss! Didn't you hear me? There was a Kaiju attack!"

Looking up to the control room, Mako Ikari sees almost her entire team trying to watch her, their faces illuminated by the glows of each cell phone causes her to shudder. The view reminds her of old horror movies. Taking a deep breath she begins pacing. "Where? I received no news about a possible sighting."

"It was here!" Carsten shouts into his phone. "Isayama attacked people--"

"--Not the tour?!" Mako asks as the colour drains from her face. "Has there been any word from Gideon?" A tiny part of her hopes that it was the group, it would mean the island would close; the assets sold off to the highest bidder while she finishes her glorious work.

"No idea," Lathrop Preston's voice echoes from the phone's speaker. "All we know is that Isayama was in the vicinity of the main power generator."

"No," Mako says. "None of them have ever shown any interest in the generator. That's why it was designed that way...Why hasn't the backup activated yet? Shouldn't the geothermic keep us constantly powered?"

She can see her team hurriedly talking amongst themselves. Some shake their heads while others use their phones, most likely doing rough calculations. *They don't know why,* Mako thinks. Most likely it's another glitch in the system due to the short time frame before opening. Mako shakes her head. "Never mind. Do we know what caused Isayama to attack? The Category 1s aren't usually aggressive."

It's Julayne Hughes who answers. "Professor, all we know is that Isayama attacked a group of people near the power generator just before it exploded. Without power, we can't do anything...Sorry."

Mako slumps to the hard cold floor as she says softly, "There's no way to track the Kaijus...they can go anywhere and we are defenceless." A loud snort causes her to spin, her eyes widening.

Ishiro's four eyes stare at Mako, the blue glow from them plunging the room into a deeper blue-violet. Above her she can hear the faint banging of her team's fists on the shatter-proof glass. She knows what they are saying and can feel the radiation emanating from the beast. Mako stares back defiantly. "What?!"

The Kaiju rears up, the enormous head grazing the ceiling and then with a horrendous screeching snarling, it roars. The sound cuts through all other noises and Mako's phone itself screams feedback at her. The woman cringes and drops the phone as she grabs her ears, her eyes darting up to the control room and she can see the team doing the same.

The sound forces her onto her back and the tiny human has to close her eyes, clamping them shut to block out the pain. She has never in her life experienced this type of sound before. Not even when she has been experimenting on the Kaijus. Her brain screams at her to make the sound stop and she can feel droplets of blood begin to come from her ears and nose.

Mako's instincts kick in and she rolls onto her stomach and begins half-dragging half-crawling away, hoping to get to a safe enough distance that the sound...

She stops and slowly opens her eyes.

Mako blinks and smiles slightly.

Ishiro has ceased his roaring.

The woman gets to her feet and looks at the monster. The gigantic head is once again resting on the floor and the four eyes are shut. The tip of the tongue slithers out and licks the nose and snout, much in the same way that a dog does. Quickly, Mako scoops up her phone and checks the screen.

"Damn," she mutters as the phone slowly reboots. "Come on!" she orders the phone but technology has always been uncooperative with her.

The instant the phone is ready she dials Carsten and barks one order, "Find out where Gideon Pryke is. Now!"

CHAPTER TEN

"Now there's no need to panic. I can assure you that everything is under control. We just have to remain calm," Gideon Pryke is in damage control mode. He looks at the scared faces of the investors and smiles. "The backup generator will switch on any minute now. Don't worry--"

Teresa Hernandez laughs, it is full of sarcasm and doubt. "He tells us to remain calm...Are you so arrogant Mister Pryke--"

"--Gideon, please."

She ignores him, "Are you so arrogant to think that you can control every situation?"

Pryke stares at her, his eyes never leaving hers as he says, "Yes my dear."

This infuriates the reporter to no end and as she opens her mouth a deep boom freezes her and the others. The ground shakes from another that sounds closer. Teresa glances at Pryke. "Could that be the power?"

Another boom is quickly followed by another, then another and another. Each one sounds deeper and is mixed with a splintering cracking sound. As if something is knocking down trees.

"I don't think it's the power," Crichton says as he points.

The small band looks, following the digit and each of them sighs, not really surprised at what they see; trees shaking and then some collapse, pushed over by a monstrous form. Through the tree-line an orange glow can just be made out.

Instinctively the investors and reporter begin backing up while Pryke steps forward and squints, trying to see better. He can barely make out scorpion-like pincers and drooling mandibles. Quickly he looks down at his wristwatch and curses, *Not enough time to power up the*

Mechs.

He turns back to the group and has to shout over the crashing, "Well the good news is that's a Kaiju. Bad news--"

"--Isn't that bad news enough!" Tull hollers. He is gripping Beacham's arm tightly and sniffs back tears and fear.

Gideon Pryke laughs. "Come now! This is Kaiju World; here we are prepared for--"

A shrill ear splitting snarl stops him. They are now bathed in the orange glow from the creature. The air around them fills with the rancid smell of decomposition and stale food.

"What I was about to say," Pryke whispers hurriedly. "Is the bad news is this; that particular one is Ifukube. One of our Category 4s."

The air is punctuated by the clicking of the larger than life mandibles and the snapping and clacking of the pincers. Pryke has never seen any of his assets up close before but he knows each and every single one of them from the images and security footage he's been shown. From all of the Kaijus, Ifukube has shown itself to be the most territorial and eager to fight. The owner of Kaiju World knows they have to, "STOP!"

Emmerich is running full speed across the open field towards the Tour ATV. All of the vehicles are button-started and no keys are needed. Which is how Pryke wanted it, but now he wishes that they had stuck with key ignitions.

Tull, seeing this also runs, chasing after his partner with a high-pitched wail. His arms flailing about like a small child.

The clicking gains speed, as if the monster is becoming excited by the fleeing men.

Pryke and the others watch as Emmerich trips over a fallen log and Tull leaps over him. It's a race to see who gets to the car first. Crichton, Beacham and Winston don't say a word but their faces tell it all; complete and utter disgust at the selfishness on display.

A smile creeps across Winston's craggy face and he says, "Five-hundred on Emmerich."

This gets a small chuckle from Crichton who replies, "Hundred or thousand?"

The bulk of a man shrugs, "Why not thousand?"

Beacham scoffs, "Really? Right now?"

Winston nudges the smaller man and uses his head to gesture at the ATV. Beacham looks and his mouth drops open. "I'm in," he says excitedly.

Teresa shakes her head and turns, looking away in disgust at the capitalism on display. "Fucking money-men," she spits with a shake of her head. "Umm, what happened to the monster?"

Pryke spins quickly, looking around trying to spot the Kaiju. He finds it hard to believe that a monster that big could just disappear. *Mako said that they all have different abilities,* he remembers. Part of him wants to run, but the adventurer in him demands that he stays and sees his prize in action.

Tull reaches the ATV first and fumbles with the door. The latch is hidden, built into the door itself; smooth and streamlined like the fuselage of a plane. "Fuck you!" he screams as he slams into the side of the vehicle.

Emmerich stands over him and lands a solid hard kick into the man's stomach. "Dummkopf," he says and easily opens the door.

Tull scrambles to his feet and grabs the back of Emmerich's shirt and pulls hard.

The larger man shakes him off and clambers into the vehicle. He tries to close the door but the other man is able to leap inside.

"What the hell are they doing?" Pryke asks.

Winston laughs, "Being themselves."

"What's that?" Teresa asks, her voice filled with dread.

The ATV roars to life, the lights blaring on, blinding everyone.

Teresa screams and Pryke starts shaking his head while the three investors' mouths drop open as they stare blankly, not fully comprehending what they are witnessing; as the two men in the vehicle struggle with the column mounted gear-shift they don't notice the enormous pincers slowly surrounding them. Tull is pointing at the column-shift and hysterically trying to get his point across while Emmerich looks completely disinterested in whatever the other man is saying.

The left deadly pincer opens and closes the closer it gets, making a soft clacking that gets louder just before it snaps shut around the rear-end of the ATV. The serrated edges easily crush the metal, the steel roll bars bending and snapping as if made from cardboard.

As the back of the vehicle is being chomped and churned, both Emmerich and Tull begin trying desperately to get out. As the younger man gets the door open the other pincer slams into it, bending the door and trapping it in the opening.

"They're gonna die!" Beacham shouts.

Pryke can do nothing but stand and watch in dreadful awe. He had no idea that the creatures are this ruthless.

"Do something!" Teresa shakes Pryke.

The owner of Kaiju World says sadly, "There's nothing we can do."

"The Mechs!" Beacham snaps his fingers.

Pryke shakes his head and turns, the screeching of the metal unnerving him. "They take too long to power up."

"Dios mio," Teresa says with a gasp.

This makes Pryke turn back, his curiosity getting the better of him. Nothing can prepare him for the terrible sight happening before the quickly diminishing group; the ATV is being lifted off the ground by the back pincer while the front tries to shred and tear the front away, allowing the tasty morsels inside to be reached.

Emmerich is pushing Tull towards the front with his feet as his arms frantically pull him back. His partner loses his grip and falls, smashing his face against the windshield.

It cracks slightly and blood splatters from the impact. Tull cries out and grabs his nose, now a misshapen lump of flesh and bone.

His eyes widen and he screams a high-pitch almost girlish howl of fright. He is staring into the saliva dripping, rapidly snapping mandibles of the Kaiju. Tull's scream is cut short as a part of the mouth bites, the mandibles slicing the front of the chassis like a hot knife through butter.

Emmerich slips then drops, his legs catching on the seat.

There is a jaw clenching cracking and wet tearing as the femur breaks and stabs through the flesh splattering the plush upholstery in dark blood as the man bounces. His body slams into the roof and he slides the rest of the way down.

The two men grab each other as they smash through the windshield. The shards of glass slicing them, their blood electrifying the monster who chitters and growls happily. The pincers lower the wrecked vehicle into the gaping maw.

Teresa looks away, her mettle having enough and the other three investors keep their eyes focused as the monster's mandibles slowly feed the Tour ATV with the screaming Emmerich and Tull inside into its mouth.

The mandibles help crush the steel frames and tear out the chairs. Emmerich tries to punch and kick the limb away but all he accomplishes is the Kaiju chittering excitedly. His bloody leg still spurts warm blood that lands on the mouth organ and with a shriek of pure euphoria, Ifukube shovels the wrecked vehicle down its gullet.

#

Dutch quickly ducks under a low hanging branch as he runs through the dense forest. His eyes constantly scanning the area for any sign of the intruders or Pryke and the tour group. *Just dumb fucking luck,* he thinks as he hears the rest of his team next to him. Each one moving as stealthily as they can while carrying heavy packs full of their custom made Kaiju hunting gear, and the normal rations needed for such a job. Dutch smiles to himself as he thinks about what he and his team will do when they find the responsible parties. *Damn the orders,* he thinks.

They were already out and racing to the beach when they heard and saw the top of the explosion. Dutch had immediately changed their objective; the boat was meaningless, the generator became the new goal. Unfortunately the outage had slowed them down since the gates in the electrified fences weren't responding to the control panels, meaning that at each one they had to waste valuable time cutting through the thick heavy duty locking mechanisms. Luckily for them, Lawrence has the perfect tools for the job and even though it still takes him upwards of ten minutes for each lock, they move quickly and quietly.

"Are you hundred percent?" Johann whispers as they stop to catch their breaths, they are covered by large trees that sway in the heavy wind.

Dutch checks his GPS map, thankful for the satellite feed. "It makes sense, logically. If there were intruders and they wanted to disrupt us then the best and most obvious target would be the generator."

"Well," Lawrence says. "When you say it like that..."

The rest of Asset Retrieval Team laugh and each checks their weapon; Roxie holds a modified Steyr AUG, instead of the standard 5.56mm rounds, this one fires lasers. Turns out they are the best for slowing down a Kaiju. All that regular bullets do is annoy the monsters. The good thing about the Steyr AUG Triple-Sec, as she likes to call it, is that it uses a continuing battery to charge the emitter. The red-dot sight helps the accuracy of the weapon as well. Lawrence carries the big gun, a modified Barrett Model 82, with once again laser ammunition, though the giant of a man does also carry a Two-Handed Katana Machete. In fact, all of the weapons carried by A.R. Team have been modified by Mako and her people to do one thing and one thing only, take down and incapacitate any and all Kaijus.

"Ready ladies?" Dutch asks, he seems more alert than before which puts the others on edge.

"Boss," Roxie says. "What's the problem? We can handle anything thrown at us," she looks at the other two men, "right?"

Lawrence smiles and pats his weapon while Johann chuckles before saying, "Well personally I'd rather deal with a nice bottle of red and some chocolate...but this'll do just fine."

Dutch smiles slightly and rubs his beard; the bristles feel good and always relax him. His eyes scan the surrounding foliage and he sighs before speaking. "The power's down right? Which means that any of the

Kaijus can be roaming about free as a bird." He doesn't finish the thought but he never has to. After trapping as many city destroying monsters as they have, each person there knows how shittier the situation can get.

"So then, why don't we go and round them up?" Roxie asks.

"That's not the mission," Lawrence says, his eyes also beginning to scan the area. "Shit," he mutters. "Wish I had brought the scanners."

Johann looks at him like he is the biggest idiot on the planet. Rolling his eyes he says, "You didn't bring them? Why the hell not?"

Even Roxie turns on the man. "You really are a drongo! What possessed you to leave home without them?"

Their tech-guru shrugs and looks to Dutch. "Sorry boss. It's just that I didn't think--"

Roxie grabs him by his shirt front and shoves him against the trunk of the large old tree, shouting, "You never think! One job! That's all you have to do. Bring the goddamn equipment we NEED!" She relaxes instantly as she feels the commanding hand of Dutch on her shoulder.

"Lay off," her CO says calmly. "None of us thought we'd be in this situation. Just imagine how everybody back at the main compound is reacting." An evil grin splits Dutch's face. "Can't you just picture how our illustrious leader is carrying-on?"

That makes everyone laugh and the tension dissolves. Dutch grabs his chest, his hand gripping the vest pocket that holds his phone. Quickly he opens it and looks at the screen. "What now?" he asks nobody and then answers. "We're in the middle of something...Really...We were going there to check it out...No...Shit...Fine!" he puts the phone back in his pocket and looks at his team. His face is expressionless as he says, "New orders."

"Bullshit!"

"Fuck that!"

"Bad form!"

Dutch hushes them with a raised hand. "This comes from McTiernan not Pryke. There is a situation, Gideon Pryke is missing and they need us to make sure that--" He stops midsentence as his phone vibrates again.

"Betcha," Roxie says, "that it's even newer orders."

They watch as Dutch reads the message on the screen. His eyes widen and he shakes his head in disbelief.

"What is it Boss?" Johann asks, equal concern crossing his face.

"Professor Ikari needs us to fetch a Category 1," Dutch says, each word tasting bad in his mouth. He continues speaking, cutting off the protests of his team, "Her preference is for Anno, but Higuchi is also fine." He quickly checks his weapon and makes sure his pack is secured.

Satisfied he looks at the constantly rising cloud of smoke and electrical discharge off in the distance and says, "We'll be her delivery boys later."

"Dutch," Roxie speaks up. "Does that mean we're disobeying direct orders?"

The leader of A.R. Team looks at his team and he half-smiles. "We're not the military."

#

James McTiernan slams his fists against the table in his small office and curses his luck, without the backup generator they are flying blind and to make matters even worse, Security doesn't know where the small tour group is or what their situation is. He knows that the moment Pryke gets back, if he returns that is, his job is gone and once again he will be nothing more than a disgraced ex-special forces agent.

He looks up and sees the control room all staring at him; they have never seen him show his emotions so clearly. *Keep it together man,* he tells himself as he looks at his phone. Dutch hasn't sent a confirmation yet and neither has Pryke or Mako.

That is the one thing that has him really concerned, the fact that there is no defined line of communications or procedures for this situation. Sure, they have contingencies for nearly all possibilities but nothing for power loss. *Better go and rally them,* he thinks and exits his office.

Donna Mixon is the first to speak, her voice ringing out loudly in the quiet room. "Has anyone been able to get in contact with S&P?" She isn't asking but giving a command. "Homer," she addresses Simpson, "get on it now."

"Yes Ma'am!"

Her eyes are daggers as she snarls, "Do I look like some ninety year old Queen?"

The young man looks unsure. "Ummm, no?"

"Damn right!" she snaps. "So whenever you address me, you will do it with 'Sir'. You get me?"

Simpson is up on his feet standing at full attention as he shouts, "I get you Sir!"

Donna waves him away and turns to Chris Winder and JR Handley who are both trying to contain their laughter. "Something funny?"

Both men stop chuckling and look like children caught acting up. Winder nudges Handley who opens his mouth, "No Donna."

"Are you sure?"

He nods and spots McTiernan. "Sir, still nothing to report. All we know is that something took out the power."

"No shit Sherlock," Donna says before turning to McTiernan. "What's the plan?"

The CO of Security looks at the expectant faces of his team and instantly worries about the rest of his people scattered all over the park. "Any word from the rest of our people?"

Winder answers, "Sir, yessir. Everyone is accounted for and ready for orders."

"Good," McTiernan says. "Do we know anything about the status of the Kaijus?"

Handley shakes his head. "Not presently."

"Okay." McTiernan looks to Robert Tillsley. "Can we do anything to get the power--"

"--Sir," Simpson calls out. He holds up his phone. "S&P are reporting that they can get power back."

The room erupts with sighs of relief and lots of whoops for joy. There is something about the young man's tone of voice that has McTiernan worried. "What else, Simpson?"

"Well...It's just that...they haven't finished writing the code for the backup power yet. All they can give us are cameras and basic communications," the young recruit answers with a grimace. He really doesn't want Donna to yell at him, or anyone else too for that matter.

"Figures," Handley mutters.

McTiernan nods. "That'll have to do for now. Thank you." He looks at his people and is thankful they are all professionals and have not panicked. "I want to thank all of you for your hard work these past years. But I'm afraid that this will be the end of Kaiju World."

"What?"

"Are you serious?"

"What will we do?"

McTiernan raises his hands. "I personally guarantee you will be given fair compensation. Each of you will receive three years pay and will be given the highest recommendation for any job you want." He smiles as some of the screens flicker to life. "Good," he sighs. "Bernardi, you Handley and Winder focus on getting a sitrep on the Kaijus. I want to know what each and every single one of them is doing." He turns to Donna, "I want you and Simpson to do everything you can to get a lock on Pryke and his guests."

They nod and set about performing their tasks while the rest of the room sits and waits patiently for their orders. Most are positive they know what is about to be said but they wait anyway.

"As for the rest of you," McTiernan says. "We will begin evacuation of the island. You know the drill, all personnel will be airlifted off the island while data and research will be uploaded to Pryke's servers. I also want physical backups ready within the hour. There is no telling--"

"--Sir," Drue Bernardi looks pale as he speaks. "I have good news and bad news."

"What now?"

"Well," Handley speaks. "It ain't good, that's for sure."

"Spit it out," Donna barks.

"Relax, Donna," McTiernan says, then waits for one of the three men to speak.

"We can't track them, that's the thing. S&P hasn't patched us in to Ikari's system yet. All we can do is cycle through the cameras until we can find them," Winder says, always the voice of reason.

James McTiernan nods, "People you have your orders. I want this island cleared within three hours. Somebody alert the mainland. We're gonna need helicopters, and carriers ASAP." He looks at Winder. "Well? Let's start."

CHAPTER ELEVEN

"Why does this keep happening?" Rick Shaw sobs as his legs threaten to give up and have him collapse.

"Maybe," Christopher Michael huffs and puffs as he weaves between trees, ferns and bushes. "Just maybe it has something to do with being on an island inhabited by gargantuan monsters!"

None of them are certain how long they've been running for. It could be minutes or hours, but either way the raging beast thundering behind them has no plans of changing course any time soon.

"I wonder," Christopher muses, enjoying the adrenaline coursing through his veins. "How can they see us?"

"Why don't you stop and ask?" Jeremy Smith calls as he narrowly misses being struck by the beam of electricity that shoots past him and engulfs a tree in blue flames.

"No thanks," Christopher shouts back. "I'm good!"

Ellen Scott's been running in silence since the Kaiju spotted them. Shaw screamed and took off, leaving her and the others looking confused. Then the taloned foot crashed down, demolishing a couple of acres of trees. The foot had thick tufts of coarse looking fur pushing up and out between the scales. Christopher had opened fire instantly, emptying a magazine of his Beretta 9mm. Jeremy pulled on him until the man realized it was a futile exercise trying to shoot through the thick scales.

Now Ellen wants only one thing; for her men to shut up so she can figure out a plan. *Is that too much to ask for?* she thinks as she feels the hair on the back of her neck stand up. That can only mean one thing and Ellen slides, looking up briefly to catch a glimpse of a lightning bolt scream across her vision.

"You sure we're going the right way?" Shaw cries over the rumbling from the Kaiju, it sounds like a coming storm.

Jeremy grunts as he misjudges a leap and catches his foot on a tree root. He hits the ground and rolls easily. Then he is back on his feet. "Positive! We keep going straight until--"

He yelps as they all tumble down a small incline; the branches and heavy leaves from shrubs slap and cut any bare skin as they tumble until they land in a pile of splayed limbs.

Quickly, Shaw crawls out from under Ellen and begins dusting the sand off his pants. "Who put that fucking there?!"

Ellen rolls and pulls the man down as a giant tree crashes down, the roots impaling the ground Shaw was just standing on. "Move!"

Running on sand is normally difficult; it gives way too easily and has the habit of trapping the foot of whoever is running on it. But when being chased by Godzilla's pissed off cousin and the adrenaline fighting for control, sand is the single worst thing to encounter.

The four members of Animal Alliance sink, slip, trip and knock into each other as they try to outrun the Kaiju.

"Thank you Jeebus!" Shaw howls as the boat comes into view.

Ellen feels rejuvenated, as do the others, and pushes her body harder. Her lungs burn with each breath she takes and her muscles are screaming for a break. She can't stop now, they must reach the boat. Though the thought of the electrical beam makes her pause; it seems like the monster can fire at will and without needing to recharge it.

Dropping to her knee, Ellen expertly wedges the four magazines into the sand and steadies her aim, holding the gun with both hands and pressing her elbows against her body.

"What are you, crazy?" Christopher yells at her.

"Get the boat into the water!" she shouts back, ignoring his question. "I'll buy you enough time!"

A rocky mountainous shadow rears up through the forest canopy. The bulbous eyes glow pale indigo and the cat-like ears swivel, trying to track the humans. It rumbles and breathes heavily.

Ellen raises the gun, her plan is to take out one of the gelatinous eyes, which she hopes will distract it long enough for her men to get off the damned island.

The air crackles and the gigantic shadow ripples as it begins sucking in oxygen. A deafening whooshing sound surrounds Ellen who opens fire, her finger squeezing the trigger again and again and again.

She has no idea if the tiny hunks of lead get anywhere near their target and frankly she doesn't care as the Kaiju opens its mouth and a bolt of bright blue electricity explodes forth. Ellen spins, following it and gasps as all she can do is watch helplessly.

Rick Shaw screams; an unholy sound of absolute pain that reminds Ellen of a wounded animal, as his insides burn and liquefies. His skin catches fire as the blast engulfs the boat, the wood offering no protection from the attack. The man's body convulses as the skin blackens, the hair on his head and face bursting into flames and the cries of anguish become hoarse as the vocal cords melt.

Jeremy and Christopher drop flat on their bellies as the boat and Rick Shaw both explode in a fiery ball of disaster that showers them with debris.

Ellen can't believe it, every single one of her plans on the island has so far failed spectacularly. The gun slips from her hand and lands with a dull thump as slowly she stands. Behind her she hears the triumphant roar of the beast as it steps out of the trees and onto the soft sand of the beach.

"Ellen!" she feels Christopher pulling her arm. "We've gotta go!"

Her mouth moves but no sound comes. Ellen wants to talk but something inside of her has given up. She is ready and willing to let the monster devour her, just to end her suffering.

Shouting and gunfire draws her back to her senses.

Blinking, Ellen sees lines of purple and red flashing through the sky, smacking into the side of the Kaiju. Each hit tears the flesh causing bright orange blood to explode and rain down onto the trees and sand.

The Kaiju screeches in pain and spins around, the tail kicking up a wave of sand.

Jeremy grabs Ellen by the other arm. "The cavalry?"

"I could hazard a guess," Christopher says with a smile. They watch as the lasers fire quicker and quicker, each one hitting the same spot causing smoke to slowly form. The grouping of shots is truly impressive; there is barely any change in where the laser hits. Whoever is firing knows exactly what they are doing.

Finally the Kaiju roars in frustration, turns then flees into the forest. Christopher whoops and fist pumps the air. "Yeah! That's how you do it!"

Faint voices can be heard approaching and Ellen says, "Leave this to me." She promptly faints just as Dutch and the A.R. Team get close; their weapons are raised and pointed at the three survivors.

"What's all this then?" Dutch asks with a raised eyebrow.

#

"Rejoice! Rejoice for I have returned!" Gideon Pryke booms as his small band of sorry looking people burst into the main hall of the resort. Expecting to be flocked by worried employees and Department Chiefs, the man is more than surprised when nobody takes any notice of him. All around them people are hurrying about, carrying boxes of documents and files, rolling racks of servers and checking tablets. The other odd thing is that the hall and staircase are being lit by work-lights connected to portable generators.

"So much for a grand reception," Winston wheezes. He is leaning against a pillar and is breathing hard. The sweat on his brow mingles with the blood from the cuts and gashes on his face.

Beacham, Crichton and Teresa look just as bad; the two men's clothes are torn and stained with already drying blood. Their faces are muddy and each man looks dazed and slightly confused. Teresa, meanwhile, has a distinctly singular expression on her face; that of wanting to murder one Gideon Pryke. Her shirt has singe marks on it and her long hair is in tangles. Combined they look perfectly miserable.

Pryke looks annoyed at being ignored by his people and he claps his hands hard. "Hey!" Nobody stops as they are all too focused on their jobs. Pryke scratches his head. "What's going on?"

"Why not try using your phone?" Teresa sneers. The sheepish smile Pryke gives her flames her anger. Part of her wishes that he had been the one to get eaten by the monster and not the two businessmen. "Where is it?"

Pryke holds up his hands. "I must've dropped it on the trek back."

"You shitheel," she says and walks over to a techie that is having trouble with the rolling rack of servers. Teresa grabs the poor man by the arm and spins him. "Phone, please." The man squeaks and hands her a walkie-talkie before pushing the rack away. Casually Teresa tosses the communication device to Pryke who fumbles with it slightly.

"What am I supposed to do with this?" he asks, staring at the twin dials on top.

"Call your Head of Security!"

Pryke doesn't like being ordered about and glares at the woman. *Definitely a mistake inviting her,* he thinks as he spins the knobs to the correct channel. *When this is over,* he tells himself, *she won't publish a single damn word.* He knows that given the chance Teresa Hernandez will do everything she can to destroy his reputation and the park. That is something he cannot and will not allow to happen. The billion and billions of dollars invested means that he personally will always be in debt, unless Kaiju World is a resounding success. *She better had signed that NDA.* "James? Come in James McTiernan?" he says into the walkie and waits.

"I need to lie down," Winston moans mere seconds before collapsing with a loud thud. Beacham and Crichton stare, stunned from the sudden fall and are late in reacting. They drop to their knees and try shaking the massive bulk but Winston is unresponsive.

"Help!" Crichton calls out.

"James! This is Gideon Pryke! There's a situation in the main hall and we need a medic!" Pryke barks into the walkie talkie, his voice is commanding and has the same tone as Patrick Stewart in Star Trek: The Next Generation.

"Pryke?" McTiernan's voice crackles in surprise. "Where the fuck have you been?"

"Get down here with medical and I'll tell you."

"Medical? What's going on...you hurt?"

"Not at all dear boy," Pryke's voice has returned to its usual easygoing tone. "One of our visitors seems to have suffered a coronary."

"On our way," the walkie talkie crackles again and Pryke looks smugly at Teresa. His face rapidly changes to concern when he sees the woman performing CPR; she is blowing air into Winston's mouth while Crichton is providing the compressions on the flabby chest.

Maybe I should get at least one signature, Pryke thinks as he spies Beacham standing to the side looking as if his life has ended. "How you doing, chap?"

Beacham glances up at Pryke and swallows his emotions before speaking. "How do you think I'm doing?"

Pryke blinks, in the twenty years he has known these men not once has he ever heard Beacham raise his voice. "I can hazard a guess," he says, placing a consoling hand on the man's shoulder. "You're not the only one to lose a friend."

Beacham shakes loose the comforting hand. "It's always about you. Isn't it?"

Gideon Pryke tries to hold back his smile and unfortunately fails. "Well...Look at--"

"--Pryke! What the hell is going on?" James McTiernan's voice stops everyone in the hall. The only sounds apart from the clacking of boots on the tiled floor that can be heard are the squeaking wheels of the server racks. Not a single soul wants to make a sound. "Well?"

Pryke smiles pleasantly and steps to the side allowing the Chief of Security and the four man Medical Team to see the unconscious Winston. "No idea," he says.

McTiernan snaps his fingers and the room erupts in movement; the techies and personnel return to their tasks as the medics race over and begin preparing the body.

The owner of Kaiju World watches McTiernan who closes the distance between them in five long steps. "James!" Pryke is all politeness. "How are you? It's been forever, I must say."

"Why haven't you been answering your phone?"

"Funny story," Pryke says with a chuckle. "So, over at Mechs Vs Kaijus...we really need to rename it...Ifukube attacked us." His smile grows bigger at McTiernan's shocked reaction. "So," the billionaire continues with a clap of his hands. "What's all this then?"

It takes McTiernan ten seconds to register the question. "Wait...You were attacked by Ifukube?" Quickly he counts how many people are standing before him. "How did you get away?"

Gideon Pryke actually belly laughs, holding his stomach he arches forward with great big guffaws. It is the first time in a while that he has properly laughed. Waving his hand dismissively he says, "Oh, I shan't bore you with the details. But suffice to say it involved some pretty quick thinking, a lot of running and using Kaiju dung."

His Chief of Security nods, he knows that he'll never get a more in depth answer and honestly he's fine with that. Glancing down McTiernan sees the Medics mumbling and shaking their heads. James McTiernan has seen so much death over the course of his life that now he can easily spot it.

"What's going on James?"

McTiernan pushes past Pryke and stands next to Beacham, "It's never good when you lose a man."

"I suppose," the money-man says with a nod.

The ex-military man nods too. "My old Sargent Major had a saying for these occasions." He clears his throat and uses his best gruff voice, "Shit happens." McTiernan turns and walks back over to Pryke. "We need to talk."

#

Mako Ikari sighs in relief for the hundredth time.

With the emergency lights and communications back on she and her team feel more at ease. That is until they receive word of Isayama's death and the attack on Pryke and the investors. Now the island's resident Kaiju expert is fighting two completely different feelings; on the one hand Mako knows that if there are, or have been any deaths then the entire project is done. There will be no appeals, no chance to prove that a freak accident had happened. Everything will instantly be shut down. But, on the other, if the situation does escalate as it surely will then she will have the perfect excuse to show the world the next stage in--

"Repeat that," she says into her phone.

"You need to get out of there!" Lathrop Preston's voice is panicky.

The Japanese woman turns just in time to scream as one of Ishiro's six feet slams into the control room.

The wall cracks and splinters, huge chunks of concrete and steel beams tumble to the floor as sparks fly and shards of glass rain down.

She watches as the mighty limb slides down the wall, each of the eight claws digging in and scraping away layers of paint and cement. Mako squints, trying to see any red blood or her team.

Her gasp is full of sorrow.

Lathrop's mangled body is impaled by one of the claw's tips. It is dragged down, the flesh catching and then shredding on the broken glass. The thick shards rip open his stomach and the bright pink intestine slowly unravels, leaving a trail of bodily fluid, acidic juices and slimy blood.

"Is anybody else hurt?" Mako screams.

Slowly she sees the rest of her team and she breathes. "What set him off?"

Julayne Hughes answers, "No idea but...Fuck!"

The foot careens into the wall again and Mako spins to look at the Kaiju.

Ishiro's eyes bore into her; judging her, challenging her and daring Mako to try and do something.

You're not like the others, she thinks as she feels fear taking over her as two of the unbelievably huge eyes slowly and deliberately wink at her. Then with a mighty bellow, Ishiro the Category 5 Kaiju rears up and begins to repeatedly smash its enormous head into the roof.

"Mako!" she barely hears the voice over the cacophony of destruction. "Mako!"

Professor Mako Ikari weaves and lunges, doing everything she can to dodge the falling debris; slabs of concrete, steel beams, ducts and bunches of wires all come down in hunks and chunks.

She yelps as the hard ground greets her.

Mako feels the throbbing in her left ankle and knows instantly that she has twisted it. She tries crawling but the roar from the beast freezes her.

As one of the gargantuan clawed feet hurtles towards her, Mako Ikari is vaguely aware of Brad Carsten's voice bellowing, "Somebody activate the damn Sedation System!"

CHAPTER TWELVE

"I don't trust them," Roxie mutters to Dutch again. She glances back at the three newcomers and frowns. "Their story makes no sense...You have gotta be fucking kidding me!"

A satisfied smile on his face, Dutch casually lets a plume of thick bluish smoke escape from his lips and nose. He sighs and holds up the big cigar. "One of life's few and only true pleasures." He takes another long puff while Roxie snorts. "Relax," he tells her.

Roxie shakes her head as she stalks ahead, her large machete blade cutting a swath through the forest. Her anger and suspicion is justified and Dutch fully agrees with her about their story, but he isn't worried about them. Why should he? He's travelled across the most dangerous places known to man; Darfur, Burkina Faso, Burundi, the Democratic Republic of the Congo, Iraq, Niger, Mogadishu and Venezuela. He's met the most terrible people imaginable and shared drinks with them. Dutch has, due to his experiences, become a walking lie detector and the moment the woman started talking, he knew something was up. But he just wasn't sure about what.

Then there was the other thing, the two men haven't spoken much. In fact they have barely said more than "Yes" and "No" whenever anyone from A.R. Team asks them a question. It is always the woman, Ellen, who speaks for them. This makes Dutch think she must be their leader... *Makes sense,* he says glancing back at them. The two men, Jeremy Smith and Christopher Michael are covering the woman as his own people; Johann and Lawrence walk slightly ahead and slightly behind them. It seems like they are just covering all possible areas but in fact they are guarding the three. "Roxie," Dutch calls. "Take five."

"About time!" Johann says with a sigh of relief. Even though he is their Equipment Master, the dark skinned man is small so for him the continuous trekking is slightly harder.

Lawrence tosses his pack on the ground and sniffs the air. "You know what they say?" He looks at the bloodied, dirty tired people then to Johann who shrugs. Lawrence smiles, "The secret of happiness is not found in seeking more, but in developing the capacity to enjoy less." The big man waits for someone to ask the follow up but pouts when nobody does. Grunting he sits on the forest floor, legs crossed and stares at the small fire that Johann has started. "Well, for any philosophy buffs here, that was Aristotle and what it means is--"

"--Socrates," Christopher says quietly. "It wasn't Aristotle, but Socrates who said it," he looks over at Lawrence. "And before you tell us what it means, stop and think for a second. Did you see it on some stupid motivational post online, or did you study it in university? Because," he raises a hand. "Because if you didn't and are just spouting it for the sake of it, better keep your mouth shut."

"Here we go," Roxie mutters to Dutch who just shrugs and continues enjoying his cigar.

"What did you say, boy?" Lawrence says slowly. He has never been questioned about his philosophical knowledge before.

"Leave it," Ellen says, pushing her arm against Christopher who is slowly getting to his feet. The man looks at his boss then to Lawrence and snorts before sitting back down next to her.

Dutch uses this moment to saunter over to the small fire and flop down, his legs crossing and the man gets comfortable easily. His eyes pass over the three newcomers as he holds up the cigar and stares at the glowing tip. "So, tell me again why you three were on the beach being chased by one of my beasties?"

Christopher and Jeremy exchange almost frantic glances then look to Ellen whose eyes have not left Dutch's face. She blinks slowly and opens her mouth, "We were on a break when the power went off--"

"--What sections do you work in?" Dutch doesn't miss a beat in asking his question.

"Christopher here works in--" she stops talking when Dutch holds up a hand.

"You," he asks Christopher directly.

"Kitchen," he says.

Dutch nods then looks at Jeremy, "And you?"

The big man plays with his long braided hair before answering, "I'm one of the tour guides." He continues talking in a monotone in answer to Dutch's expression, "I was able to get early access so I could get used to this place."

Dutch smiles slightly then stares at Ellen.

"Reception in the hotel," her tone says it all and she leans back, crossing her arms waiting for the next question.

A distant rumbling makes everyone look up; Dutch and the rest of A.R. Team hold their weapons ready, their fingers resting on the trigger guards. Ellen, Christopher and Lawrence huddle closer together, though Ellen has a slight smile playing on her lips. She hopes that if it is a Kaiju than these fools are taken while she and her boys can get away.

"Boss," Roxie says, inching up next to Dutch. "What do we do?"

He knows what she is talking about but right now he's preoccupied. *They are probably the idiots who put us here,* he thinks listening to his gut and instincts. *Better to kneecap and leave 'em for the beast.* He shakes his head, trying to get rid of the old ways. "Everyone," he says, his voice deadly calm. "Do exactly as I say and we might get out of this in one piece." His jaw is tense and his teeth cut into the tobacco leaf.

Ellen stands and stretches. "It's just the storm coming in. We'll be fine--"

Her voice is drowned out by the roar. Unlike the other ones this sounds metallic, as if chains were being dragged across sheets of plate metal. The sound grates on everyone's nerves and Dutch knows who is challenging them. "Fuck me," he moans.

"Is that?" Lawrence asks, his voice shaking slightly.

"Murata," Johann whispers as his finger switches the safety off.

"Who's Murata?" Ellen asks.

The roar sounds again but this time it's closer and definitely louder. The metallic scraping is now mixed with a deep rumble and a shriek, the sound reminds everyone of a car crash but this is going to be much worse.

Dutch spits the cigar into the fire and squints. "Lawrence, get into position. We need at least a one hundred head start."

The man nods before jogging away, disappearing into the jungle.

"Who is Murata?" Ellen asks again this time grabbing the bearded man's big arm.

"If you did work here," Dutch says slowly, "then you'd already know."

The air above them shatters with the piercing scream of projectiles zipping over their heads.

"Get down!" Dutch screams as the roar sounds again.

The trunks of the trees splinter as thousands of prickly spines impale themselves into the wood. Each one is longer than a basketball player and one side is covered in small serrated blades. Tiny slithers of wood and bark rain down on the people as wave after wave of spines are fired at them.

Roxie lays flat and gently squeezes the trigger of her laser rifle. The bright red bolt zooms through the forest and vanishes. She waits to hear a roar or squeal of pain. When nothing happens, she curses and rolls over to Dutch. "What's the plan?"

"Do what we do best," is all he says.

#

Gideon Pryke sits completely still and listens intently to James McTiernan as he finishes the debriefing. The owner of Kaiju World is silent and unblinking, as if he has been attacked by Medusa. The only movement is a slight nod of the head periodically and a shifting of the eyes. They are sitting in McTiernan's office; it was easier to go there instead of Pryke's own which hasn't been finished yet. Sitting on the table between them is a bottle of warm Sake and two cups. It is unopened which surprises the Chief of Security, he has never known his employer to leave a bottle closed.

Pryke still hasn't spoken a word or given any indication that he's been following the conversation. "Gideon?" McTiernan asks. "You okay?"

The sigh is long and filled with exasperation and Pryke rubs his face. "Let me get this right...Isayama is presumed dead, but there is no definitive way of telling? Why is that?" His voice is quiet and his original accent is clear. "Don't we have drones?"

"The winds are too strong for the small propellers."

"Goddamn it!" Pryke smacks the table with his hands, the dull thud echoes in the small room. "What's the point of all this technology," he gestures at the equipment sitting just outside, "if we can't do a damned thing with it?" It is a rhetorical question and the billionaire philanthropist continues speaking, "Okay, let's say for arguments sake, it is dead...Emmerich and Tull are gone too..." He looks at the roof and thinks before finally speaking, "We are totally fucked."

"Don't forget the supposed intruders," McTiernan adds helpfully.

"Oh, thank you for reminding me," Pryke's voice is dripping with sarcasm. "Pray tell, who is responsible for the security of Kaiju World?"

James McTiernan knows full well where Pryke is heading. He has gone through this talk before with the other rich and stupid men he has worked for. Not this time. "With all due respect, Sir," his voice makes Pryke look up. "But you've been in such a rush to get assets here, that certain vital things have fallen by the wayside."

Pryke blinks, "What did you say?"

"You heard me," if McTiernan is going down, then he will go down guns blazing. "You wanted constant drones surveying the island, which would have been a good idea except for the storms we get. You were told the island had blind spots and that we needed triple the number of security cameras already installed. But as always you said 'No'. That was the pattern; anytime we gave you alternatives to any of your ideas to make this the most advanced theme park. Your answer was always the same...Everything that is happening here, the deaths, all of it is on you."

James McTiernan is towering over Gideon Pryke who has trouble meeting the Chief of Security's gaze. The tapping at the door gets his attention and a curt nod lets Donna Mixon know she can enter.

"Sir," she says ignoring Pryke. "More reports are coming in. Ishiro tried to escape containment and almost killed Mako Ikari. Also--"

"--Is she okay?" Pryke interrupts.

"Also," Donna refuses to acknowledge the other man's presence, "we've been able to track the Kaijus and...well...Getting anally fisted by a telephone is going to be more fun."

"You do know I pay your salary?" Pryke really hates being ignored.

"My apologies," Donna says as he hands her CO a small file. "Do you want a medal?" she says leaving the office.

McTiernan flips through the file, his eyes skimming each page rapidly and slowly his shoulders slump. "Shit, we need more time," he mutters.

"What is it?"

"The Kaijus are heading for us and Containment," his voice is hollow and empty.

"So?" Pryke says. "We're evacuating, right?"

McTiernan shakes his head. "The helos coming from Chiba are going to be at least four hours. We've got maybe two, tops."

"Why is it going to take that long?"

The Chief of Security chuckles and shakes his head sadly. "As with nearly anything involving the Japanese government, they will need to hold countless meetings to discuss every single thing they can do. If we are lucky it will only take them three hours to make a decision."

"Bollocks," Pryke says. "What can we do?"

"Not a lot," McTiernan replies as he stares at his people. "Unless you can get in contact with some private military contractors? If not, then we're going to need weapons, something to keep them at bay long enough."

Pryke snaps his fingers as he leaps up. "Where's A.R. Team?"

A slight press of a smooth button on the table brings up a display.

"Here." McTiernan points to a spot on the map of Maikeru Island. "That was their last known position."

Nodding, Pryke points to another spot. "The Mechs aren't that far away."

"No."

But Gideon Pryke is already on his phone. McTiernan lunges and tries to grab it but his boss moves. "Don't Gideon. It's a stupid move."

Pryke looks confused as he puts the phone to speaker, "Dutch? I say, Dutch, you there?"

The sounds coming from the small device's speaker is heavily distorted, the small drivers struggling to reproduce the sounds clearly, but what the two men can make out does not fill either of them with much confidence; humans screaming and crying out, inhumane roars and snarls that are similar to the banging crashing of construction and also the high-pitch cable swaying twang of lasers.

"Dutch?" McTiernan shouts at the phone.

Both men strain to decipher the terrible sounds. McTiernan has heard similar noises before which makes it easier for him; to his trained ear A.R. Team is in the middle of a losing battle.

"Down! Now!" Dutch's voice cuts through the distortion. His voice is drowned out by a roar. "Move!" they hear him bellow as the twanging and pinging of lasers can be heard. It is quickly followed by a shrieking and then an explosion that cuts them off.

Slowly, Gideon Pryke looks up at James McTiernan. The billionaire's smile is one of pure excitement. His Chief of Security shakes his head emphatically. "No!"

"Sorry old chap," Pryke says as he quickly scoops up the phone. It clicks and buzzes as his fingers dance across the virtual keyboard. "Righty-o."

"What did you just do?"

The owner of the island and the park places the phone back on the table as his eyes meet McTiernan's. "Buying us time."

"What did you do?" McTiernan's voice is filled with dread.

The pleasantness of Pryke's voice surprises the other man, "They're going to get the Mechs."

"Shit," the Chief curses with a shake of his head. "Do you have any idea about the destruction you've brought down on us?"

"You said it yourself. We need to buy time--"

He flinches as the phone crashes against the wall, smashing into pieces. McTiernan breathes hard as he speaks, "You don't use gasoline to put out a fire! What you've done," his voice is barely controlled, "is unleashed three robots on us. They are going to do far more damage than the Kaijus by themselves. I commend you for wanting them to protect us but in a fight against the monsters, the chaos that will be caused is going to be multiplied exponentially."

McTiernan wipes his brow and swallows before continuing, "Each of these has been outfitted with advanced military grade weapons. There is no guarantee, and you know how much I like guarantees, on exactly what will happen, but if you are willing to--"

Both men look around as the entire complex shakes violently and the lights flicker as the power fluctuates. Pryke goes to the door and stares out at the Security Team who are not fazed by the tremors.

McTiernan stalks past Pryke and says softly, "Mister Pryke, you have killed us all. Hope the show will be worth it."

#

The ground shakes and rumbles from the force of the thrashing Ishiro. His back is riddled with small tranquilizer darts that have thin lines of orange blood trickling down the sides of the Kaiju. It whimpers, straining at the enormous chains and restraints. The gargantuan monster's constant struggling and crashing about has almost destroyed the containment hangar, the wrecked jagged metal and concrete stabs and cuts into the flesh.

"Why isn't it down?" Julayne Hughs asks as she wipes tears from her eyes.

Mako Ikari stares at the carnage around her. She looks at all of the smashed equipment, the cracked displays sparking and fizzing with the electricity still pulsing through the cables. Her eyes keep avoiding the dead mangled bodies of her teammates lying in pools of blood. "Who's dead?" she asks softly.

"Sean Campbell, Yudhanjaya Wigeratne...Lathrop Preston and Paul Cooley," Brad Carsten says as Julayne wipes and cleans a large ugly gash on his forehead.

"And Walters," Julayne adds.

"Michael?" Mako says as her body mourns the dead. *Our hubris,* she thinks knowing that Gideon Pryke will be helpless to save Kaiju World from closure.

"Professor? What is it doing?"

Mako slowly goes over and looks down at Ishirio. Its eyes stare up at the wrecked control room; they are frightened and are pleading with them. The clawed feet scratch the metal floor, each large talon leaving long jagged grooves.

From the back of the monster, bulging pustules begin to rise and fall with the rapid breathing of the Kaiju. There seems to be something underneath each one, as if Ishiro was mutating.

Mako watches for a few seconds more and then looks at the remains of her team. "Can we track them?"

Carsten shakes his head then winces from the pain. "It's all busted." He cocks his head to the side, almost positive about why she would ask...almost that is. "Why?"

As Mako opens her mouth, the wall mounted phones and the hand-held radios in the room scream to life, the sudden onslaught of tones startles the researcher, professor and scientist. Without a word, Mako Ikari answers the closest phone. "Kon'nichiwa..."

"Mako?! Thank god." It's Pryke. He sounds relieved but his voice still shakes slightly.

"Mister Pryke?"

"Gideon," he says. Even during a cataclysmic disaster he still prefers a casual atmosphere.

Mako grunts slightly, her eyes refusing to leave the still whimpering creature. "Gideon we have a --"

"--We're evacuating the island," he talks over her. "The Kaiju are on the move and..."

Her mind drifts as it all makes sense. *Ishiro wants out,* Mako thinks with a small gasp. *The Kaiju can sense the movement of each other!*

"Mako? Mako!" Pryke screams into the phone.

"We're trapped, for now," she says calmly. The sudden realization of what is happening and the opportunity she has fully relaxes her. "Don't send anyone."

"Are you out of your mind?" Pryke is genuinely concerned and slightly confused at the same time.

"Not in the least, but they might say I was," Mako's answer is cryptic but Pryke can hear the smile in her voice.

"What are you planning?"

"Project Robinson," is all she says. Carsten and Julayne exchange inquisitive looks, but neither speak.

Pryke whistles, impressed. "Are you positive that now is the time?"

"No Gideon," Mako says, looking at the writhing beast below. From the pustules she can see what looks like the beginning of tentacles begin to push forward. Each one pops the bulb and thick blood mixed with golden white pus flows freely. "But what other choice do we have? The Mechs will surely fail, then what?"

She can hear Pryke nodding on the other end of the line. "Fair enough, which one?"

"Anno or Higuchi."

"There might be a problem with that," Pryke says as Ishiro screams in panic. The remaining lights hanging from the roof swing wildly as dust drifts to the floor and more cracks begin spider-webbing across the ceiling.

"Don't tell me," Mako sighs, the calmness slowly leaving her. "They're dead?"

"Pish!" Pryke is dismissive as he continues. "A.R. Team is fetching us the Mechs."

"You have got to be kidding?" Mako says as Ishiro's roar shakes the room. The lights darken and there is a hiccup in the phone's connection which cuts them off. The woman hangs up the phone then picks it up, trying to hear a dial tone but getting nothing but a steady clicking.

"Everything okay?" Carsten asks, his voice full of concern. He and Julayne have been trying to clear some of the rubble so they can get out of the room.

Before their boss can talk, Julayne almost shrieks, "What's Project Robinson? Is it a way out of here?"

Mako sighs. "It's just something that Pryke and myself have been working on. A just in case if anything should go wrong."

"What could possibly go wrong?" Carsten laughs. "Spit it, boss. What are you planning to do with the Kaijus?"

Mako Ikari looks at her people then to the thrashing gigantic beast. She wants to tell them everything but she knows what their reaction is going to be. It will be the same as when she first told Gideon Pryke, he had said she was mad. But in the end Mako was able to convince him. Now though, there is no time so instead she sighs and talks, "We need to release him--"

"--What?!"

"That is the second stupidest idea after cake in a cup," Carsten says with a snort, both instantly forgetting all about Project Robinson.

Their boss shakes her head and stumbles as the compound shakes and trembles violently. Another shrieking roar from Ishiro shatters the remaining windows, glass screens and shields.

Julayne's eyes are wide, panicky and her voice trembles slightly as she says, getting to her feet, "What good could it do?"

"The others are coming, probably to attack us and Ishiro," Mako says using the same tone as Dutch or McTiernan. It surprises her, this reservoir of strength. "We don't have enough time to get out," she says while glancing at the panic filled Kaiju. "But there should be enough to..."

"No," Julayne declares as she redoubles her efforts to clear the rubble. "We can make it!"

A tearing, shredding, cracking, deafening cacophony of destruction forces the three humans and the Kaiju to stop what they are doing; Mako races over to the edge of the smashed opening and holding onto a hanging cable she watches, mouth hanging open as large jagged cracks begin to spread across the walls and roof.

"We can make it!" Julayne screams again as a large slab of the roof above her crashes down. Her scream is cut short as the heavy concrete lands on her, the weight crushing her bones and her face being shredded by the edges. Her eyes go blank as the life is pushed out of her and the immediate area is splattered with her blood.

Brad Carsten howls and races to the ruined body, he grabs the dead woman's hand and pulls, trying to save her. He pulls and the limp limb comes off with a hideous sickening wet rip. Carsten sobs, dropping the hand and then collapses onto his back. His tears mix with the blood of Julayne's and his vision is blurred by his sorrow. He does not see the exposed wire that is flipping and whipping about, moving closer and closer to his leg.

The death howl of Brad Carsten causes Mako to spin her head and she gasps at the sight of her comrade convulsing about. He looks like he is doing an involuntary breakdance demonstration but the smoke rising from his body says otherwise. Carsten's mouth clamps down and his tongue drops to the floor in a bloody mess. Mako steps towards him but stops as another loud smash makes her flinch as the cracks in the walls split open.

Shafts of light show the true amount of destruction caused by Ishiro in his panic. The entire hangar is never going to be rebuilt. Mako sighs then screams as she falls through a fresh hole just as a gigantic red eye glares in through the new cracks and a series of snarls and growls fill the chamber. The Professor can make out Ishiro's body, it is now covered in writhing and undulating tentacles. The sight makes her want to vomit.

Ishiro's eyes become slits as it stares at the red eye and it snarls as the jowls around the mouth curl into a smile.

CHAPTER THIRTEEN

"We really going for the Mechs?" Roxie asks as they near the Mechs Vs Kaijus arena. They haven't seen any sign of Murata since he ambushed them about an hour ago. The Kaiju had become distracted the moment they got close to the wrecked generators.

Quickly, Dutch glances at the small ragtag group and counts the odds. *It'll be close,* he thinks then shrugs saying, "We're paid to do one thing."

Roxie knows what's coming and doesn't bother letting the man finish. "Obey orders."

"Atta girl," Dutch says with a friendly pat on the arm. "Besides," he says, "would you rather go after Anno without one?"

"I'd rather be on a Cuban beach with a mojito and not a care in the world," Roxie says. "But if wishes were horses--," both tense up as the sound of pounding footsteps crushing dried leaves comes up behind them. They spin, weapons springing up ready to annihilate the would be attacker.

"Scheisse!" Johann curses, breathing heavily while adjusting his pack. "You trying to kill me?"

"Apologies," Dutch says lowering his gun. "It's getting hard to see without the lamps," his apology is weak but honest. With the approaching darkness and no power to provide light, any sudden movements or loud noises amplifies the tension everyone is feeling.

"What's up?" Roxie uses her question to stare at Ellen, Christopher and Jeremy; each one is trying to wipe away fresh blood from deep gashes or trying to figure out how to stop blood flowing. "Our friends causing problems?"

The Austrian shakes his head dismissively while catching his breath. "Not yet." He holds up a couple of Polaroids making both Dutch and Roxie raise their eyebrows, they cannot remember the last time a Polaroid had been shown to either of them. Johann ignores their surprise, "Not a word." He clears his throat. "It wasn't a Kaiju or a power surge."

Dutch takes the photos and quickly scans each one. In the distance they hear roaring and the tell-tale sounds of a building being demolished. The bearded man purses his lips. "You positive?" It's a redundant question to be sure and Dutch is almost positive that Johann is correct, but he is and always has been a firm believer of better safe than sorry.

The look Johann gives is priceless. "See these dark marks?" He points to four dark circular patterns that have jagged edges that look like clouds. "IEDs or C4," he says with the authority of a seasoned professional.

"C4?" Roxie asks, taking the photos.

Dutch stares at the sky then to the newcomers, he has this nagging felling at the back of his mind. It is similar to an itch that, unfortunately, the man cannot scratch. "Do you really think it could be an IED?"

Johann nods and shakes his head at the same time as the distant roars and crashing draws their attention. "Is it her?"

Both Roxie and Dutch nod, their faces grim. "We get the Mechs then split up," he says. "Roxie, you and Johann will go back to Control and save the day." He's moving fast now and the others have to race to keep up with him.

"What do I tell Larry?" Johann asks as he tries catching his breath again while almost running at full speed.

"Nothing," Roxie says. "Just give him a warning but nothing too overt." She glances at Dutch. "What about you?"

As they come into the clearing that is overshadowed by the ancient Aztec-inspired looking temple and the four railgun armed security towers that are powered down, the wind dies leaving the group in nothing but eerie silence and stillness. Dutch is wary as he steps out into the open, he knows that they are going to be exposed to an attack and if one of the Kaijus is in the area then they are all well and truly fucked.

"Boss?" Roxie asks. She and the others are standing at the tree line, waiting to see if any gigantic monsters rampage over and tear the man to shreds.

He waves for them to follow as he takes off at a fast jog over to the almost ridiculously sized hangar. Dutch looks at the industrial automatic roller door then grabs the bottom with both hands and pulls up. His muscles bulge but the door barely moves an inch. Grunting, he bangs on it with his fist in frustration.

"Problem?" Ellen asks. She is pressed flat up against the wall and seems to have been re-energized by the sight of the temple.

He grunts before answering, wondering where Roxie is. "The door." He doesn't want to waste time since he still doesn't know what to do with these three.

"We can get it open," the woman says and without another word Ellen, Christopher and Jeremy take off running around to the backside of the hangar.

"Shit!" Dutch curses, part of him wishes that there was one of the smaller monsters waiting for them. He smiles slightly at the thought of them being torn asunder by the giant teeth. *If wishes were horses,* he thinks as from inside the hangar he can barely make out the sounds of feet running across the hard cement floor.

"What the hell?" Lawrence demands as he stalks up to his CO. "Where did they run off to?"

"When you got to go," Johann says with a chuckle. He flinches from the hard hit to the shoulder from Roxie. "What?"

She rolls her eyes. "Any excuse to make a Jurassic Park reference."

"What can I say?"

"Quiet!" Dutch hisses. He has his ear against the shutter and his eyes are slits of pure concentration.

"What? Did we get fucked?" Roxie asks as her finger flicks the safety on her weapon off.

"Possibly," Dutch says as he forces all of his auditory facilities to focus on the hollow nothingness inside the Mech hangar.

"Why are we even here?" Lawrence asks impatiently.

"Because the man who signs the checks says so," Roxie responds.

The answer isn't good enough by any standard for Lawrence. "But doesn't he know that--"

He is cut off as the metal roller door buckles with a bone chilling creak then is ripped apart as if the steel was nothing more than tissue paper. The man looks up, mouth agape at the gigantic plate covered robotic arm that has punched through the door.

"Move!" Dutch orders as the plated gear driven hand grips a sharp edge and begins pulling.

Metal scrapes against metal and the sound pierces the ears of A.R. Team. Each member of the highly specialized unit running, trying to get as far away from the hangar as possible.

"How?" is all Lawrence can say when they reach one of the towers.

"It doesn't matter," Dutch is in combat mode. He knows that the Mechs are almost as deadly as the Kaiju, almost; after all they had been built to fight. But, luckily for him and his team there is a ten millisecond delay between a command being given and the robot performing it. This is more than enough for them to do some real damage. "Can you get this going?"

Johann and Lawrence both look up at the railgun. "Give us time...Yeah!"

Dutch watches as the two men begin the climb. Then he turns to Roxie as they hear the door being torn from its tracks. "Let's go hunting."

She nods and quickly checks her weapon; the ammunition counter reads as having a full clip. Roxie smiles slightly and raises the gun, tucking the stock under her shoulder and holding it tight. There is no need to do this since lasers produce no recoil at all as there is no combustible powder in the rounds, but old habits die hard. "What's the plan of attack--"

The gun slips from her fingers as she stares at the three slowly rising robots. Each one has a distinct style to the armour plating and shape; the smallest of the three has a small loping gait and the way the body is shaped is reminiscent of a sumo wrestler. For some reason the designers gave it a rotund mid-section. The second one is tall and lean with a swimmer's body shape. Its head has a small fin on top of it giving it the appearance of a shark hybrid. As for the third and tallest of the lot, its body is covered in thick plates of armour, just like a knight.

Each one struggles slightly to get to its feet, the size and weight giving the inexperienced pilots inside some trouble as the joints and gears are stiff from non-usage. The groaning from the movements is loud and reminds Dutch of an antique clock that needs oil. His hands shake slightly; there is something off-putting about the faceless mechanoids as opposed to the Kaijus. The monsters have faces that grin, grimace, frown and show emotions, the blankness of the robots is unnatural.

"Boss," Roxie whispers. "Do we have a plan?"

The Knightbot's head turns slowly; the blank staring visor for eyes seems to focus on the two small people. There is a crackle of static and a loud booming feminine voice erupts from the built in speakers. "Thank you kindly, Sir!" The Mech performs a very awkward bow as the voice continues, "Animal Alliance wishes you all the best, and...well...Toodles." A shaky hand gesture and the three twenty-five story tall robots turn and begin heading towards the ocean.

Dutch raises his weapon, the gun begins to hum and the barrel slowly glows. "Aim for the ankles." He doesn't wait for Roxie to answer as his finger squeezes the trigger.

The smaller Sumo-Mech stumbles as the lasers ping and bounce off the armour, it turns and raises one arm, the limb slowly rotating and transforming; the fingers slide back as the palm opens, revealing a cannon. "Fuck!" Roxie screams as the plasma blast hits the ground just in front of her, the pale blue plasma vaporising the ground, the grass and the dried leaves.

Dutch's eyes dart to the tower where he can just make out the two men waving their arms and pointing at the three robots. *At least they haven't been spotted,* he thinks as another plasma blast sends him flying.

He lands hard and he gasps for breath, his left hand searching for the gun as the other prods his chest and ribs. Nothing feels broken. The sounds of lasers being fired makes him focus and the man can't help but smile.

Roxie stands prone, her legs slightly apart and at right angles. Her face is a defiant roar and the lasers bathe her in a hazy strobe effect. Each hit does little to no damage but she groups each shot perfectly, aiming at the plasma gun on the hand. "Are they ready yet?" she hollers as her thumb hits the recharge button while she leaps out of the way of yet another blast.

The answer to her question is a high-pitch whining that is quickly followed by a bolt of lightning that takes out the midsection of the attacking Mech. Its arms swing limply and the head twitches moments before the robot topples forward, collapsing on the ground.

From the tower, Dutch and Roxie can hear their teammates cheer. They watch the railgun swivel, the two men manually aiming the impressive weapon.

"Clever!" Ellen's voice booms from the Mech in Knight's armour. "But it won't save you." The hand leaps up, pointing.

Dutch is able to duck, yanking Roxie to the ground as a Kaiju crashes into the clearing. It's a round ball that wobbles slightly. "Anno," the man whispers. He hopes that the Category 1 is strong enough to take down the remaining Mechs.

Anno growls and the same slit in its mouth begins tearing across the body as large nasty sharp teeth become visible. It roars then moves with surprising speed, the monster leaps into the air then comes crashing down on top of the downed robot.

"Christopher! No!" Ellen's voice rings out as the Kaiju rolls back and forth, crushing the mechanoid into the ground. It stops and a large ruby red wet tongue slithers out and licks the face, savouring the flavours and taste of victory. "Damn you!" Ellen sneers and unleashes her Mech's weapons.

Anno shrieks in pain and panic as blue flames engulf it. The creature tries running but the flames hold it in place.

"Jeremy!" Ellen barks.

The Sharkbot slams into the crying Kaiju, lifts it up high then with a mighty throw hurls the living ball into the air.

Everyone freezes, eyes tracking the blue flaming monster as it sails, a trail of burning flesh carried by the wind following. It seems to hover in the sky, like an odd star, then Anno smashes, colliding into the stone on top of the temple with a dull squishy wet thud.

"Shit fuck," Roxie softly curses after recovering from her shock.

"I'm going to keep this," Ellen Scott booms.

Dutch is smiling and chuckling as he dusts himself off. Roxie glances at him. "What?"

"There's a reason," the man is laughing hard now. "I wasn't too happy with--"

The shriek is distorted and Ellen's Mech thrashes as a leathery engorged head sucks and nibbles on the robot's own head. Claws dig into the shoulder joints and the air is filled with the foul stench of melting metal.

"Higuchi," Dutch says happily as he and Roxie watch the dislocated jaw working the head and torso. Acidic drool drips and instantly begins melting away the plate armour.

Jeremy's Mech stands there awkwardly, unsure of what to do about this new attacking Kaiju currently trying to eat his boss. Over the comms he can hear her screaming and crying out for help, but the man is too afraid of his Gods. Never in his life did he think he would ever see something like this up close. His mind cannot handle it anymore.

There's a loud hissing of gas as coolant is blasted from vents and the head opens, revealing a cylinder cockpit that is then launched, projected high into the sky.

Roxie cannot believe her eyes as the escape tube slams into the temple and explodes in a small ball of flames. She laughs then quickly remembers where she is and what has just happened.

"Boss!" Johann calls as he and Lawrence run up to the two while Higuchi starts shaking its enormous head. The monster is trying to rip off the domed head of the robot so that it can continue feasting on the innards.

"Good men!" Dutch says and claps hands with Lawrence and then Johann. Behind them, the Category 1 lifts its head in triumph and roars. It is muffled by the severed head in its mouth. The gigantic throat begins pulsating as the muscles work, then with a wet popping sound both it and Ellen Scott inside disappear.

"Fucking Mechs," is all the bearded man says.

#

"Oh god," Mako Ikari whimpers as she cowers behind a section of fallen roof. Covering her ears, the woman squeezes her eyes shut tightly. She forces her mind to go to her happy place and not let the memory of her family's death come to the front, which is impossible as all around her Ishiro battles the Category 3 Tanaka and Category 2s Kayama and Nakajima.

The thunder of the heavy beasts mixed with their roars and shrieks of pain cuts through Mako's hands and her memories fight to be relived; her father had heard on the news about a coming eruption from Mount Fuji. He wasn't worried, he never was and that would be his downfall. The Japanese Authorities had closed public transportation and the schools so little Mako had a few days off from school. There they were, all playing and having fun when the first earthquake--

"No!" Mako screams, forcing herself to look at the Kaijus.

The only other times that she's seen these mighty gargantuans battle has been via the drones, security cameras and the movies of her youth. It's always looked exciting but up close and in real life?

Each of the smaller monsters launches itself onto Ishiro's sides and back. Claws dig into the flesh and act like hooks while fangs and horns try to cause as much damage as possible. All that Ishiro can do is roll, using its own immense weight to crush the attacking beasts.

The newly birthed tentacles, meanwhile, whip and flick the more pedantic Kaijus. Each one is launched with a wet sucking sound as the suction cups let go. The rest are pummelled into the ground until they are nothing but masses of bloody orange pulp.

Kayama squeals and thrashes on the ground, impaled by a large column of steel, wires and cabling. With surprising speed one of Ishiro's tentacles whips about, grabbing the wounded Kaiju, then tears it from its stake and hurls the screaming beast across the hangar where it crashes through one of the cracked and fragile walls.

The impact rips the wall from its foundations and it topples, exposing more of the outside world in a thick cloud of dust.

With a deafening roar that shakes the building, Ishiro's back begins to glow a deep red that pulses and slowly grows brighter and as it does the skin begins to heat up and steam rises from the body.

The lights erupt from the cracks in the skin, beams of light that cuts through any and all that gets in the way. Nothing is safe from the beams as steel and concrete melts away, instantly making the building shake and groan.

The slightly smaller Kaijus leap away, narrowly avoiding the beams. Limbs, tails, horns are all disintegrated and the Category 5 is washed in orange blood and viscera.

Mako crawls, trying to avoid being crushed by the massive bodies or the falling debris. She feels the intense heat from the light beams and knows that the room and probably the hangar and most of the compound are being exposed to dangerously high levels of radiation.

What were you expecting? she asks herself as Ishiro's head thrashes about, the limp bloodied head of Kayama in the powerful jaws. There's something about the way Ishiro's eyes dart about, not erratically but they move as if they are looking for something...or someone.

Ishiro howls as claws tear at one side of the humongous face, scratching and pulling at the skin. The orange blood oozes slowly at first as the claws dig in under the skin becoming jagged hooks, then with a sudden exploding release a large chunk of flesh is torn from his face.

Tanaka howls in delight, watching the blank stare on the Category 5's face. It takes a few seconds for the beast to register the attack and when it does, the howl of anguish almost breaks Mako Ikari's heart.

The woman risks standing and her mouth drops open; the eyes...two of the eyes are missing, all that is left are bloody clumps of flesh with exposed bones. The tendons, veins and shreds of muscles throb as the blood oozes and seeps out. Ishiro shakes its massive head and stumbles about as a fountain of blood erupts from the open wound, spraying the walls, rubble, other Kaijus and Mako.

The beams of light shooting out of the massive back dim then disappear, while the eight legs, gigantic claws and tentacles all scrape then rip up the rubble and knock down more of the structures with a terrible screeching howl of pain.

Mako ducks and prays that she will make it out alive as her instincts take over and she runs, making a beeline for the belly of the thrashing monster. *This is crazy,* she tells herself as the shadow of the beast covers her.

Please don't collapse, she prays as her legs keep her dancing about, keeping under the Kaiju and not slipping on the pools of bright orange blood.

The tail whips about, knocking down the other Kaijus and then the feet stomp them, shattering bones and forcing them to pierce the scales and thick leathery skin. Ishiro is slowing down, calmer but now the attacks and the way it is actively trying to bring down the Containment Hangar is methodical.

The power begins to falter causing the lights to flicker, the destruction finally taking its toll.

Mako ducks and weaves as the eight legs constantly move, rising and falling in an erratic rhythm. To her it seems like the Kaiju is looking for something or someone--

She yells as her foot gets caught and the blood catches her, smothering her in its gooey grasp. Mako can feel the air being pushed out of her and panic sets in. Around her she can feel the Kaiju fighting, the thundering and the roars are muffled and everything is distant to her. *This isn't my time,* she repeats to herself as she struggles to move, trying desperately to find a way out.

Then the weight of the world comes crashing down on her back and Mako Ikari wants to scream, has to scream but now her world is only one thing.

The orange blood.

Everything is now the suffocating, sulfuric smelling, orange Kaiju blood.

And there is no escape for her.

CHAPTER FOURTEEN

Teresa Hernandez looks around the medical ward of Kaiju World. It wasn't what she was expecting at all, but then nothing she has witnessed today has been anything she could ever expect to see, except for in a movie.

If she had to describe the large oval room she is standing in, the only image that comes to her mind is the Sick Bay from the latest Star Trek movies. *He really outdid himself with this,* Teresa thinks as she has to squint slightly. Every single surface is polished white and shines blindingly in the bright overhead lights. The entire Medical Ward is the perfect definition of Ultra-Futuristic. Teresa cannot help but wonder how much it all set him back.

"What's going on?" a young doctor asks frantically as security guards, each of them dressed in light blue coveralls with a utility belt, begin to wheel out patients. With the constant shaking and power fluctuations, the place has been having more customers than any of the medical staff had expected, especially since they haven't opened yet.

"You can't move him!" the doctor shouts, trying to stop the guards from removing the covered mass that was formerly Winston.

The guard shakes him off then expertly unlocks the gurney's wheels. Crichton grabs the large man's arm. "Who do you think you are doing this?"

"Robert Buckels. We're evacuating and this corpse is not on my list," Buckels says before shoving the other man out of the way.

Teresa helps Crichton off the floor. "Did he say we're evacuating?"

"I believe so," he says as his eyes watch the scene. There are more security guards who are busy removing the valuable equipment. The doctors and nurses follow demurely, nobody wants to be left behind.

"What's that?"

Teresa cocks her head. "What's what?"

It's coming from outside. Faint. Almost undetectable to the ear, but it is still there. A deep rumbling that could easily be mistaken for thunder. The only problem is that the rumbling is getting closer and louder. "That," Crichton says with a slight shiver in his voice.

The people scream in fright as the lights flicker on and off as a high pitch whine threatens to deafen everyone.

"Alright people!" Buckels barks. "We got word of a possible incoming bogey. What I need all of you to do is--" he stops midsentence and his mouth does nothing but flaps open and shut.

A second later the wall behind him explodes as a bright beam of light cuts through the tiles, wiring and steel support structures.

Crichton grabs Teresa and pulls her down to the floor as more beams slice through the Medical Ward. All that they can hear is the whooshing of the beams mixed with the terrified wailing of the staff.

A terrible roar stops every man and woman in their tracks. The noise slowly fades away and both Teresa and Crichton have heard something very similar, even though they don't want to admit it.

"We've got to get out of here," she whispers to the man.

"You think I don't know that?" he snaps as his eyes dance across the room, trying frantically to find a way out that doesn't include leaping across a fiery chasm.

Metal shrieks and groans as something large pushes on the walls.

"How thick do you suppose—" Teresa's voice is drowned out as a large claw tears through the wall. It is quickly followed by another claw that rips another section of the wall.

High shrieking winds blow the paper and loose bits of debris about as both Teresa and Crichton try running from the gigantic monster.

From the corner of her eye the woman can see five security guards with large long cattle prods that have been customized. They attack the claws, shoving the sparking tri-pronged ends against the hard skin.

From outside they can hear the monster shriek as the claws disappear.

"Stay sharp," one of the guards orders as the small team moves into the middle of the wrecked room. They form a small circle, back to back so that they cannot be taken by surprise.

Unfortunately, none of the highly trained personnel notice the tips of the Kaiju's tentacles slowly begin to creep in through the fresh scratches.

Crichton and Teresa do and they want to, they have to, they must shout a warning. But one of the guards spots them and gestures for both to be quiet and stay where they are, completely oblivious to the wet death creeping towards them.

"What the..." one of the guards says as he feels suction on his leg. He looks down and screams at the horrid sight.

The rest of his team spins and each instantly starts to attack the slippery tendril. Their weapons sparking each time they make contact with the thick wet skin. At each contact the guard howls and dances about, his body being thoroughly filled with enough electricity to power a small city.

The body cannot take any more of the power and explodes in a bloody pulpy mess. Bones shoot across the room and impale people, stabbing into the chest or face and nailing them to the walls.

The security team are thrown to the ground and some roll, trying to put out the fires that are covering their bodies. The others feel nothing except for the tentacles. They wrap around the bodies and slowly begin to squeeze.

"Now's our chance," Crichton mutters while pushing Teresa. They jump over the bodies and tentacles as they race for the door.

Behind them Teresa can hear the men cry out and she hazards a glance back. For the rest of her life she will never forget the sight; the tentacles are dragging the men back towards the openings. The poor souls can do nothing but moan and sob at their fates.

The fat of each tentacle bulges slightly as it has to fight through the gouges but they eventually pop through. This speeds up the retreat and soon the first man is being pulled, the suction cups gripping tightly and the pressure slowly building. Their faces swell up and turn maroon as all of the blood is forced to the heads.

Their eyes bulge and the tiny veins all begin to explode. Every single one of them in the poor man's body all rupture then explode, flooding the cavity with red and white blood cells.

The tentacles have to fight with the body and the constant back and forth is too much on the bones, which snap and crack. The organs are all being displaced and forced up into the rib cage, compacting the lungs and suffocating the men. Their sobs become hoarse and they can do nothing but pray for the release of death.

Teresa Hernandez doesn't see the bodies collapse or explode from the tentacles but she does hear the muffled cries.

#

"Professor!"

"Professor Ikari?!"

"Fuck, she looks dryer than a dead dingo's sack."

The voices are becoming louder now, like someone is slowly turning up the volume on a TV. The woman's voice is the loudest and most clear, cutting through everything else and forcing the darkness, that suffocating darkness which is so welcoming to her, reaching out and embracing Mako Ikari to retreat.

"This looks like the aftermath of a Michael Bay movie," an accented voice jokes and the darkness is replaced by a bright burning light.

"Professor Ikari, are you injured?" that voice! Mako knows that voice, it's soothing and commanding at the same time. The voice is masculine and reminds her of her father.

Slowly Mako opens her eyes and smiles before wincing; she is lying on her back with her head in the lap of a smiling black man. She squints and begins coughing.

Dutch helps her to sit up and gently pats her back, helping to force the remnants of the sticky blood to be heaved up and expelled from the small woman's lungs. "Glad to have you back," Dutch says with a big genuine smile.

"Not sure about that," Mako sputters, trying to spit and get rid of the taste. Never in her life has the Kaiju expert ever tasted anything like it in her life. The only way she can describe the flavours is a mixture of cigarette ash, boiled cabbage, stale milk and dried blood. Mako knows that it is going to be a long time before she will be rid of it, but for her it is totally worth it.

"You'll be right as rain in no time," the woman, Roxie, says as she watches the short man go through the wreckage.

"Boss," the accented man, Johann, speaks as he stands. "I don't think it's a good idea to hang around. Know what I mean?"

Dutch nods, everyone knows what the man is talking about. "Not until we finish our delivery."

"What on earth happened here?" the bald man, Lawrence, asks as he stares at the clumps of flesh.

Mako rubs her head and feels her body scream in pain, she gasps and begins to lie back down on the hard floor. The three people around her quickly grab her arms and gently pull her back up. Roxie says, "Can't have you going back down Prof, need to check you out."

Dutch and Lawrence walk over to Johann while Roxie begins to examine Mako. One of the first rules set down by Dutch when everyone was brought into A.R. Team was that nobody asked about past jobs or lives. What mattered was the skills everyone has and how it can be utilized in the capture of Kaijus. But the fact that Roxie has the skillset of a world-class doctor at her age has the rest of the team questioning her past continuously.

"Bet she killed a man in surgery," Johann says with a smile.

"Nah," Lawrence shakes his head as his boot kicks a blank staring eye that is bigger than him. "Nobody died--"

"--Is this really the time?" Dutch's voice makes it clear that this is the last time they bring it up.

"You're probably right," Johann says as he stares at the scorch marks that cover the majority of the cement, steel supports and light fixtures. "What the hell happened?"

That's the question that is bugging Dutch, he hasn't seen this sort of destruction since Burma and the randomness of it all sends a shiver down his spine. "An escape," he mutters.

"The Cat Five?!" Johann gasps as he stares at all of the mounds of flesh and pools of blood.

Lawrence is nodding. "Isn't it obvious?" He gestures at the carnage around them. "The others probably came to visit him and...well..." He doesn't need to finish the thought as the other two men have already put it all together.

Johann whistles, "How did she survive then?"

"That's the sixty-four dollar question," Dutch says. His instincts are screaming at him to check on their prize for the Professor, but something about all of the destruction and carnage makes him pause. "Check on the delivery," he orders as he strides over to the women.

"You don't remember a single thing?" he hears Roxie asking for what he thinks is the tenth time; the exasperation in her voice makes that perfectly clear.

Mako shakes her head. "Just the fighting."

Roxie nods then glances at Dutch. She shakes her head slightly before speaking, "A mild concussion. Nothing serious though."

"Professor," Dutch's voice is low. "A word please." He turns to Roxie. "Make sure it's ready."

She nods then smiles slightly, reassuringly at Mako before jogging towards one of the openings. Mako looks up at Dutch. "What?"

"Did you release it?"

Mako blinks, startled by the question. "What?"

"Did. You. Release. It?" Dutch says each word slowly and deliberately.

The woman shakes her head and laughs. "Why would I do that?"

"Desperate times..."

She snorts then turns away so Dutch cannot see her eyes begin to tear up. "I'd have to be a lunatic to let that thing loose. The power it has is...is..."

"Uncontrollable," Dutch finishes her sentence with a sigh. He's heard it all before and is tired with his employers always underestimating the asset. He scratches his beard, not because of any itch but for the time it gives him before opening his mouth. "We got one."

The news brightens her day and Mako cannot help but smile. "Bring it in! Who did you get?"

Dutch holds up a hand silencing the woman, his face is unreadable as he says, "Anno...But first things first." His tone has become serious with a hint of danger to it.

The bearded leader of A.R. Team continues speaking, cutting off Mako before she can talk. "What are the contingencies for an escaped Kaiju?"

"You," is all she says.

He laughs, "Figures." Dutch isn't surprised by her answer, it seems that since Asset Recruitment was created, Pryke intended for them to always be the contingency. He sighs and his eyes notice something peculiar. "Professor did the Cat Five do this?" Dutch is pointing at the scorch marks. "What are his abilities? Can we--"

"--Dutch!" Roxie's voice echoes with terror

As Mako begins to run towards the gigantic opening in the almost ruined building, Dutch grabs her arm and spins her. "Cut the bullshit! What's the plan?"

Professor Mako Ikari shakes off the hand with a slight sneer as she says, "You're on a need to know basis, Dutch. And I'm sorry to say this, but you don't need to know."

His eyes bore into her and his voice is flat as he slowly speaks. "My people risk their lives for you. For Pryke. For this place. You can damn well tell me what is going on...Understand?"

Even though Mako knows that this man is more dangerous than any of the Kaijus on the island there is a part of her that does not want to tell him, not because she is afraid of what he will say but just in case he wants to be a part of it.

"Dutch!" Roxie shouts again.

"Enjoy the rest of your life," Dutch says as he starts walking away. "Which is going to last about five minutes."

She gets his meaning instantly and is convinced that he would leave her with the rampaging monsters. "Project Robinson!"

CHAPTER FIFTEEN

"What the blazes is going on?" Gideon Pryke looks around, his hands clamped to his ears as the klaxons blare. The sound would be deafening if not for the thundering and faint sounds of explosions from outside. All around him the Security team act cool as ice. Each man and woman are busy, not frantically, packing up the Security Control Room; powering down the computers after backing up all of the data. Checking weapons which are a mixture of standard military rifles, automatic weapons and handguns while the rest are the retro-fitted laser weapons used by A.R. Team. "Excuse me!"

"Pryke? You still here?" James McTiernan looks surprised to see the owner of Kaiju World still standing in the small office. "Hasn't anyone escorted you out yet?"

"Actually, now that you mention it," Pryke says with that off-hand tone that irritates people so easily. "They did thirty minutes ago. What you're looking at is an astral projection, perfect isn't it?"

"Handley! Winder!" McTiernan barks, ignoring Pryke's attempt at humour. He looks at JR Handley and Chris Winder who take four steps to get to the office and salute; each man is tall and their bearing screams commandos. "Take Mister Pryke to the Evac point and while you're at it, pick up his guests," McTiernan says.

"Yessir," Winder says.

"Sir," Handley snaps off another salute then turns to Pryke. "After--
"

He never gets to finish his sentence as a bright beam of light cuts through the roof of the room. It slices through his head and it takes a second before the fountain of blood spurts from the seams of the dead man.

The room shakes and the body slides apart, the insides have been cauterized by the beams.

"Look out!" screams Simpson as four more beams slice and dice their way through the control room. Panels explode in bright flashes of sparks and fires engulf men and women. The young man's cries are muffled then silenced as his body is burnt to a crisp instantly.

"Pryke, move!" McTiernan shouts, grabbing the petrified man's arm. The room is filled with a roaring tearing as the wall is crushed before collapsing; toppling into the darkness revealing the gigantic clawed covered hand of Ishiro.

"Move!" the two men pull Pryke to his feet and shove him into the hallway as the hand reaches into the room, its mass forcing the wall into a bigger opening. The entire place is shaking and trembling like a Point 8 earthquake has hit them, which would be better. At least then they could run and hide.

Behind them they can hear the crushing and smashing of the consoles and the trapped people being splattered against the walls. Pryke has gone into shock and is moving only because he is being dragged. Without McTiernan and Winder moving him, the man would have laid down and let the inevitable happen.

A beam of light slices the hallway and the three men can hear the growling of the monster. "Get word to everyone," McTiernan's voice is relatively calm, he's in combat mode. "We need to get out of here now! Anyone straggles; they can deal with the big guy."

Winder nods before screaming. The hole in his torso spurts dark red blood from the open wound that has been punched into him. McTiernan looks at the hunk of metal that lies at the man's feet and doesn't need to say anything. He knows that Chris Winder is dead.

There is an electrical scream and all of the lights go out. Only flames and sparks illuminate the hallway and for a moment McTiernan is disorientated.

"Where...where are we going?" Pryke mumbles.

"The fuck out of here."

"But.."

"Shut up and move!" McTiernan orders with a hard shove that keeps his soon to be ex-boss moving. If the man gets left behind then he'll end up like the rest of his team; Nathan Pedde - dead. Drue Bernardi - dead. Robert Tillsley - dead. Donna Mixon, he saw her face get torn off by one of the claws. All of them are dead and gone. He has no idea who is left and if the other areas of the building have been attacked. It doesn't matter since Kaiju World is officially closed two weeks before it opened.

That makes him laugh and his voice bounces off the tiled walls.

"What's so funny?" Pryke asks. The silence and movement have woken the man up and now it seems business as usual. "You think this is funny?"

James McTiernan tries to hold it in but he is becoming hysterical. "In fact, Sir, it is. This entire situation is so FUBARed that the only response that makes sense is to laugh...Unless you have an idea--" The fireball cuts him off briefly as they watch a section of hall melt away.

"This is going to cost me everything," Pryke mutters before slipping in a puddle of blood mixed with coolant.

"Boo-fucking-hoo," Crichton mutters as he and Teresa clamber through a hole in the wall. Both are bloody, covered in scratches, cuts and bruises, and are looking fed up with the place. "At least you are still alive."

McTiernan frowns slightly. "How the hell did you get here?"

"We were on our way--"

Ishiro's roar fills the hallway and the floor under them cracks. Teresa Hernandez glances down at it then at the walls and roof which are all cracking in large patterns of spider webbing. "We better keep moving," she whispers while slowly backing into another hallway.

McTiernan watches the cracks sliding across the walls and the hairs on the back of his neck stand straight up. "Don't move," he orders as a low rumbling fills the area. It's getting rapidly louder and louder until everyone's ears are filled with the roaring.

"What is that?" Pryke howls.

His words are followed by a shriek that makes them spin. Teresa is bleeding from her mouth and coughs up more dark blood. She is holding onto the tip of a talon that twitches. Her eyes go blank as her body is ripped in two.

"Holy hell!" Crichton screams as he takes off, running for his life as the hallway around him crumbles into flames. He ducks and weaves trying to avoid the beams of light cutting everything in its path. The man huffs and puffs as this is the most exercise he has ever gotten in his entire life.

"It's tracking us," McTiernan says softly as he realizes what Ishiro is doing. *How can a Kaiju track us?* he thinks as they give chase to the fleeing investor. *There is no possible way,* a part of him refuses to believe it, but the proof is crystal clear. He can hear the sharp intake of breath from Pryke as the top of Crichton's head is sliced off by a beam of light. The man stumbles slightly and slowly reaches up and touches his head. His fingers probe the exposed, slightly pink soft flesh that is his brain. He giggles childishly then flops to his knees as blood slides down the sides of his head.

"What have I done?" Pryke asks no-one in particular. There is something in his voice that makes McTiernan pause. They are both leaping across the collapsed fragments of the floor while not getting caught by the beams or the probing claws.

"Keep quiet and move," McTiernan says as they turn towards the stairwell. A person like Gideon Pryke would go for the elevator even though it is certain death, but in this situation, everything could easily become a death-trap. But they need to get out of the building and hopefully meet up with any other survivors...even one would be a miracle.

"The common curse of mankind," Pryke says. "Folly and ignorance be thine in great revenue!" he finishes and stumbles on a dead body. His panicked yelp causes the hall to groan.

"Shut up!"

Pryke chuckles. "I beg your pardon m'lord. But mayhap you could enlighten me as to where we are--"

The Security Chief rubs his knuckles as he stands over the fallen Pryke. The billionaire is rubbing his chin, the bruise already beginning to form from the punch. "Cut the bullshit," McTiernan snarls. "I need you focused and here. One...What the...?"

A low humming surrounds them, it is deep, almost like thunder but there is an electrical buzz to it that puts the ex-military man on edge. Quickly he grabs Pryke and yanks him to his feet. "We need to move, now." He's getting tired of repeating the same order time and time again but it seems that Pryke has given up. As the two men stumble along, the humming grows louder until it is all that they can hear.

Pryke cries out as they are engulfed by a pale blue light. He pushes himself off one of the cracked walls and launches down the hallway. McTiernan looks down and almost screams himself; he can see the skin on his hand slowly fade away. It doesn't melt or vanish, but just fades as if someone had slid down the fader. Then his muscles also disappear before the veins and nerves follow, then all that remains are his bones. *This isn't happening,* McTiernan tells himself as he hears a deep loud snorting and snuffling behind him.

Slowly the large man turns as his hand grabs the small walkie-talkie on his shoulder. His thumb presses the talk button as he stares into two of the large unblinking eyes of Ishiro. The communicator screeches with static and the man says, "This is James McTiernan, to anyone listening, Control is down! We need immediate help. If you see Ishiro do not--"

The roar cuts him off and McTiernan can feel his body being covered in warm sticky saliva. It's an unholy smell that invades every part of his sinuses, the smell of decaying meat that has been stuck in the teeth for god knows how long. He gags and McTiernan knows that he needs to vomit, that is all that is going through his mind. He glances down at his belt and the holster.

All he has is a small handgun that he is more than positive won't do shit to the massive monster leering at him. If he's lucky then the bullets will do only one thing, enrage Ishiro even more and make it kill hm quicker. *Fat chance of that happening,* he thinks.

In the distance he can hear the cries of Gideon Pryke and James McTiernan knows that they are all totally doomed. Nobody is coming to save them, the evacuation has failed and all the people on the island are dead, dying or soon to be dead, causing him to sob and raise the weapon.

It's his favourite, a Beretta M9 with laser dot sight and an extended clip. He's used it since the day he became a Commanding Officer and has never been without it. Mako and her people did offer to retro-fit it so that it would be more useful against the Kaijus, but he had refused. *Dumbass,* he thinks as he raises the weapon.

Ishiro roars as the tiny 9mm bullets bounce disgracefully off the thick hide. To the monster they are nothing but nuisances, but one grazes the soft tissue under the eye and the screech of pain makes James McTiernan smile.

McTiernan sighs before shouting, "Fuck you!"

#

The world is on fire.

Maikeru Island burns as the Kaijus run rampant across the small land mass; they barrel into the security towers and checkpoints without even noticing the tall structures that bend and easily impale the massive monstrosities while exploding into balls of fire and thick dark smoke billows into the sky.

Energy beams, blasts of fire and bolts of electricity dance across the trees causing the foliage to catch and burst into flames, giving the island a red orange glow of destruction.

Mako Ikari readjusts the straps holding her in and then double checks the controls. They are already moving fast and she needs to make sure that nothing happens to dislodge her. If she falls then the kill switch kicks in and everything powers down. This is good for safety but terrible in a combat situation--

"Shit," she mutters. As a beam of energy passes one of the railguns, the air crackles around it and for a second the professor worries that it has been destroyed. Over the radio she can hear people in Control crying for help as Ishiro continues destroying the facility. Mako smiles as she lines up the shot and gently presses the trigger on the right joystick.

There is no hum or whine as the two railguns, one mounted on either side, rapidly unleash their ammo. Higuchi, the Category 2, squeals before its head explodes in a fine mist of orange blood, the bone and brain matter rains down, following the collapsing body.

"Great work!" Mako whoops and looks down, below her she can see the rolling thick hide of Anno. It doesn't acknowledge her presence, the Kaiju isn't supposed to. Once the harness and control dome are mounted onto the beast, all control is given to the pilot, or as Mako calls it Kaiju-Rider.

Where the hell is Pryke? she thinks, looking at a digital overlay that shows the compound and the tiny red dots of the remaining personnel. Everyone has a tracker on them, in case of any emergency but naturally, Pryke has removed his.

Anno leaps off a cliff and lands heavily, the trees shaking then falling as Mako pushes the Category 1 harder and harder with the left joystick. Her eyes scan the readouts of the Kaiju's health, ammunition levels and the status of the weapons. Everything is reading normal, and she sighs in relief.

"Mako?" Dutch's voice comes in through the headset she is wearing.

"Yeah?"

"What's your ETA?"

"No idea," she says honestly. "I'm still getting used to the controls and Anno isn't being helpful."

Dutch's tone is deadpan as he says, "What were you expecting? The sudden ability to talk with it?" Her silence says it all and he laughs. "This isn't some anime series or bad SyFy Channel movie."

"I know that," she says as she presses the button to launch flares. They fly into the sky and distract the bigger Kaijus that are converging on Ishiro's location. "It would just be nice though."

"Nice doesn't exist in reality," Dutch says in a matter of fact tone. "All you can do is hope to survive. And honestly, you'll need all of that hope. We're about twenty minutes...Keep moving!"

Mako knows he's yelling at the rest of his team, but the order pushes her. "I'm sorry," she says to the Kaiju and flicks a switch.

The beasts screams then roars as a mixture of adrenaline, cocaine, steroids and ephedrine is pumped into its veins and directly into the bus sized heart. Mako feels the sphere of flesh speed up and she now has to fight for control, the joysticks barely registering any movement other than the weapons. "Dammit," she mutters.

"Problem?"

"Just fighting with Anno," she yelps as a large scaly spike covered foot slips on the dome.

"Well it's your project," Dutch says. "Shouldn't you have all the bugs ironed out?"

In a perfect world it would be so, but Mako Ikari has only been able to divert limited funds from her main budget to get Project Robinson to where it is now. That has been the biggest hurdle for the side project, trying to convince Pryke that eventually Kaiju World would fall and that Project Robinson is the only way to recoup the losses.

Her idea was simple, outfit the Kaijus with controls so that a person would be able to pilot it. Mako's reasoning was that the future of the world was bleak and that it would go out with a whimper, not a bang. Project Robinson would guarantee that whoever ran the Kaijus would control the bang. The only problem was that Pryke didn't fully believe in the project.

Looking at the dome, everything around Mako is only prototypes and the neural control system is at least twelve versions too primitive. But as Dutch said to her, "Desperate times."

"Where are you?"

She checks her digital map. "About five minutes away...Oh my!"

Anno has stopped and Mako is able to see the extent of the destruction and damage caused by Ishiro. The Japanese temple-looking building has been totally demolished and is nothing more than smoking rubble. Atop it stands Ishiro itself who is battling the smaller monsters. The beams of light shoot out of its back in rapid pulses as the glow from its two good eyes covers everything in the eerie x-ray.

"What is it?"

"I can see...the remains..."

"Are you sure?" Dutch's voice is full of concern. "Tell me what you see?"

"It's all gone...fire...smoke...the Kaijus are battling. Tearing at each other for...territory!"

"Can you get any readings on survivors?"

Mako opens her mouth but instead of speaking she cries out from the flash of bright pure white light. It radiates out from the centre of the Kaiju battles, enveloping everything in its way.

Is it a bomb? Mako thinks as she keeps Anno steady. Below her she can hear the small Category 1 whimpering and quivering with fright. *Why isn't there an explosion—*

Her thought is quickly lost as both she and Anno are thrown by the shockwave. They are buffeted about and the explosion is deafening. Anno rolls back and forth, trying to keep steady and Mako has to shield her eyes. The Perspex dome is cracking from the blast and she needs to know what caused it; the reactor? The underwater volcano? Or was it one of the Kaijus?

Slowly the light fades and the sight is total annihilation; all the earth is scorched and charred while the trees have been vaporised. What were once buildings are now nothing more than black husks that topple with the wind. Mako has seen images of this type of devastation before. In school they were shown pictures of the aftermath of the nuclear bombs dropped by the United States, Hiroshima and Nagasaki...but there weren't any jets or detection of missiles. Then...?

She pushes Anno on, slowly moving across the barren wasteland. In her ear she can hear Dutch's voice crying out for anyone to contact him. Were they caught in the blast? Mako hopes not because as she and her Kaiju get closer, she can see the frozen, stone hard encrusted remains of Ishiro. It stands tall, the perfect statue. The frozen Kaiju is the perfect ode to chaos and destruction; its face contorted into a snarl that is going to last forever, the tentacles are in various positions of attack and defence with some in the middle of tossing away the smaller monsters. Ishiro is covered in small ashen figures, the other Kaijus.

Was it a self-defence mechanism? Mako is enthralled by the sight.

"Mako!...Mako!"

She touches her ear, "I'm here Dutch. This is incredible."

"We saw. Are you okay?"

Mako nods then realises that he cannot see her. "Yeah, but I don't think anyone survived that." She presses a button and a square appears on the cracked dome. It zooms in on the stone-looking tentacles and Mako Ikari gasps. "I found Pryke," she sighs.

Gideon Pryke is now nothing but an ashen figure being held tightly by a tentacle. One of his legs is in the mouth of a Kaiju and his face is one of pain and terror. Nobody will ever know how he ended up in that predicament, but Mako knows his pain is over as a gust of wind blows him away, his ash floating away into the sky.

"Yeah, well it's tragic," McTiernan says. "But we got word. Choppers are inbound. Get to the beach ASAP, I'm sending you the co-ordinates now."

"What about Anno?"

Dutch sighs, "Not our concern after this. Word is that Japan is going to carpet bomb the island. Wipe every trace of Kaiju from the face of the earth. You've fifteen minutes."

CHAPTER SIXTEEN

"Do you think she'll come?" Roxie asks, pacing up and down the beach.

"Hey! Watch it!" Johann says trying to protect the red and green flares from the sand her boots kick up.

"Huh? Oh, sorry."

They got to the beach sooner than Dutch had thought. Without any of the Kaijus to worry about attacking them it was an easy trek. The only thing to slow them was Lawrence; in the blast he had been thrown against a tree. But he was able to keep up with the steady pace Dutch set for them. Even though they were positive that the coast was clear, Dutch wasn't going to take any chances and they moved with the same level of alertness they used when on a hunt.

Now at the beach all they have to do is wait for the Evac Helos and then Dutch can worry about a new job. A moan makes him look down at Lawrence who is holding his side. The makeshift bandage is oozing blood and it is obvious that the man is going to die, unless he gets medical attention soon. "You doing okay?"

Lawrence smiles weakly. "Fine and dandy."

McTiernan nods and smiles. "Good man." He's always hated leaving men behind, but sometimes life is a bitch and that's the only thing to do. Otherwise you risk the safety and wellbeing of everyone else, and as Spock said perfectly in Wrath of Kahn, "The needs of the many."

"She'll make it," Roxie says with a definite nod.

Johann groans then snaps, "Why is it so important--"

"--What's that?" Dutch says silencing everyone. He stands and raises his weapon, aiming it at the trees.

"The wind?" Johann says, quietly hoping for nothing but that. He's had enough of the gargantuans and wants to be back in his Alps.

There is a roar followed by the trees bowing and bending as Anno explodes onto the beach. The dome is cracked and Mako looks frazzled but she waves at them then points behind her.

"What the...?" Dutch says and uses his communicator. "Mako, we can't hear you. Repeat."

Her answer is to hold up the headset which is now in three pieces. She begins miming what looks like a tyrannosaurus rex stomping around and roaring, then a small ball bouncing and being kicked. Dutch and his team stare blankly at her then at each other, none are champions at charades.

"Did she hit her head?" Johann quips before ducking the right hook levelled at him by Roxie.

Mako spins in the dome, the railguns following as do the rocket launchers. Her shoulders bunch as if she is waiting for something.

"Oh no," Dutch says as his eyes widen and the realisation of what's about to happen hits him full force. "Lock and load!"

But he's too late.

The railguns and rocket launchers mounted on the smaller Kaiju open fire as Ishiro's bulk crawls through the trees. The monster is covered in exposed wounds that ooze bright orange blood, chunks of flesh dangle in the breeze and the two good eyes are nothing more than black orbs of rage, exactly like a shark.

It looks as if the monster had to tear itself from its frozen stance; the legs and what could be called arms are nothing more than slowly bleeding stumps and mounds of pulpy flesh. Bright white shards of bone are visible here and there. The question of how Ishiro has been moving is answered as a loud sucking and popping sound echoes out into the sea.

"Of course it's got tentacles," Roxie says as the tentacles dig large clumps of sand out from under the heaving bulk then toss it away. Others of the long sticky suction cupped covered limbs dive into the sand and pull. The entire motion does one thing, drags the behemoth across the sand as it roars.

The Category 5 flinches as bright explosions bombard it. Dutch and his team look at the smaller Kaiju and Mako on top.

The bolts from the railguns sear the flesh, the sizzling sound fills the ears and the smell of burning meat is mouth-watering.

"Is it weird that I'm feeling hungry?" Johann asks as he rolls, narrowly avoiding a tentacle.

"Shut up ya drongo!" Roxie answers with a laugh.

Mako continues firing, her fingers alternating between the railguns and the missiles which do nothing but to agitate the monster. Ishiro utters a low guttural growl that turns into a shriek as the beams of light converge towards its immense head.

Anno launches itself just in time to avoid the beam that shoots out of the gargantuan mouth. The tiny humans drop to the ground and feel the air vaporise above them. *If that thing ever fired in a city...*Dutch thinks before rolling to his feet.

He watches as the smaller Kaiju continues its flight and the gigantic slit of a mouth ripping open, the teeth ripping a chunk of flesh off that makes the Category 5 shriek in pain.

"Open fire!" Dutch barks as he squeezes the trigger.

Roxie whoops as she drops to her knees and squeezes the trigger of her Stygr, she has set it to automatic mode and the only thing she has to do is aim. The bolts of energy travel across the beach almost faster than light and dissipate the moment they hit the flesh. "Shit," she mutters as three tentacles shoot out at her.

Johann shouts a battle cry as he flies over to the woman, the machete in his hand making short work of the slimy tentacles. For his size he certainly packs a punch as it takes only one blow to sever the writhing limb.

"Thanks," Roxie wheezes as the Austrian helps her up.

His answer is to grin broadly then roll as more tentacles chase after him.

"Roxie!" Dutch's voice grabs her. "Back in the game!"

She nods then turns, suddenly aware of a new more familiar noise.

Behind them they can hear the low whumping of the helicopter blades. Anno does too, spinning to see the new threats and in the split second its attention is distracted, Ishiro's tentacles snap out and grabs the ball. The smaller creature howls and squeals in pain as its body is slowly crushed as the increasing number of limbs encase it and Mako inside.

Dutch takes careful aim and begins firing. The purple lasers hit their target perfectly each time, but the tentacles will not release or give. He curses and wishes they had one of the rocket launchers. *Who'd have thought it?* he muses as he leaps out of the way of a flying tree. *Who would have thought that a Category 5 would be so painful to deal with?*

He hears Roxie panting as she slides across the sand and in one smooth movement scoops up the Beretta M9. Quickly she checks the ammo counter and smiles at the triple digits. Her eyes glance down and she frowns, Lawrence isn't moving at all. His face is locked in a serene smile but his eyes are glassy.

"Stop lollygagging!"

The order breaks her momentary mourning and with a growl she drops onto the sand, the weapon resting on the body. Roxie adjusts the scope until the tentacle covered dome is in her sights then with a slight exhale, she fires.

Inside the dome, Mako Ikari panics and presses every button, squeezes the triggers on the joysticks and hopes that some weapon will force the tentacles loose. She isn't sure how much longer the dome will last but the Professor is certain that Anno will be crushed any second now. The whimpering is heartbreaking and the woman looks down, the flesh is being pushed, the mounting pressure forcing veins to burst and explode. Orange blood oozes and seeps out of the pores.

The cracking of the dome stops as all around her Mako hears the twanging and pinging of lasers mixed with the shrieks of Ishiro. Slowly the tentacles loosen their grip then drop off. Blue lasers continue to hit the tentacles, but it is too late.

On her monitor Mako sees Anno's life signs barely registering, it would take a miracle for the little ball of flesh to be okay, and she knows that there is no escape for her. She has only one last option to at least buy the others some time--

Mako Ikari screams as the broken and limp Anno is dropped into the gaping drool dripping maw of Ishiro. The massive teeth tear the flesh and bones, revealing the pulpy mess of organs that begin to slither out of the hole. Ishiro purrs as it swallows then gently places the carcass into its mouth, chews and then swallows the remains and the Professor easily.

The enormous beast ignores the laser blasts that seem to do no damage of any sort. The eyes focus on the helicopters approaching, then to the ocean and the tiny dots of light that is Chiba.

"Don't let it get to the water!" Dutch bellows as the monster's tentacles pull then acts like springs, launching the Kaiju into the air.

One of the helicopters is smacked by a tentacle and the sudden impact damages the tail rotor.

The pilots inside frantically try to restart the rotor but they are spinning wildly out of control. The other helicopters try to dive out of the way.

"Pull up!" a pilot cries out as the first smashes into it, the rotor blades dicing the protective window and tearing the two bodies apart. Both begin spinning out of control as the blades become caught, then stuck and break apart while the petrol lines rupture.

There is a spark of electricity from the black box which ignites the gas.

The explosion blinds the remnants of A.R. Team, they have to shield their eyes and look away. Around them they hear the distinct sound of something on fire plummeting to the ground.

Johann is the first to look. "Move!"

They dive out of the way of the falling burning wreckage that was the helicopters. It hits the sand with a thud and continues to burn. In the air the other helos dodge and weave, trying to avoid the tentacles. One is grabbed and the blades fly off, impaling the back of the monster.

Dutch, Johann and Roxie stand in disbelief as the Kaiju dives into the water, taking the helicopter with it and then disappears into the murky depths of the Japanese Sea. The ripples from the water displacement turn into tidal waves that converge onto the beach.

A.R. Team are barely able to make it to the trees as the sea water rushes onto the dry sand, covering everything then washes back out to sea, the wrecked helicopters taken with it.

There is nothing that they can do as behind them the sounds of burning fires eating away the forest and structures across the tiny island. Each of them knows what lies in store for the island nation of Japan and if Ishiro is not stopped, then the whole world. If only they had a way to warn the Japanese Government and the people about the approaching storm.

As the water becomes calm and mirror-like again, Dutch is the first to speak. He utters a small single sentence that sums up how they are all felling. "Shit."

THE END.

ACKNOWLEDGEMENTS

This book wouldn't be in existence if it wasn't for King Kong, Godzilla and the rest of this wonderful larger than life monsters of the silver screen. Also a massive thanks should go to my wonderful publisher Severed Press and to the Dead Robots Society Podcast and it's Listener Facebook Group.

Also By The Author

Big Smoke: Book 1 of the Apocalypse Virus

Cabins: A Short Story

Flicker

 SEVEREDPRESS

 facebook.com/severedpress
 twitter.com/severedpress

CHECK OUT OTHER GREAT KAIJU NOVELS

MURDER WORLD I KAIJU DAWN
by Jason Cordova
& Eric S Brown

Captain Vincente Huerta and the crew of the Fancy have been hired to retrieve a valuable item from a downed research vessel at the edge of the enemy's space.
It was going to be an easy payday.
But what Captain Huerta and the men, women and alien under his command didn't know was that they were being sent to the most dangerous planet in the galaxy.
Something large, ancient and most assuredly evil resides on the planet of Gorgon IV. Something so terrifying that man could barely fathom it with his puny mind. Captain Huerta must use every trick in the book, and possibly write an entirely new one, if he wants to escape Murder World.

KAIJU ARMAGEDDON
by Eric S. Brown

The attacks began without warning. Civilian and Military vessels alike simply vanished upon the waves. Crypto-zool-ogist Jerry Bryson found himself swept up into the chaos as the world discovered that the legendary beasts known as Kaiju are very real. Armies of the great beasts arose from the oceans and burrowed their way free of the Earth to declare war upon mankind. Now Dr. Bryson may be the human race's last hope in stopping the Kaiju from bringing civilization to its knees.
This is not some far distant future. This is not some alien world. This is the Earth, here and now, as we know it today, faced with the greatest threat its ever known. The Kaiju Armageddon has begun.

 SEVERED**PRESS**

f facebook.com/severedpress
t twitter.com/severedpress

CHECK OUT OTHER GREAT
KAIJU NOVELS

ATOMIC REX
by Matthew Dennion

The war is over, humanity has lost, and the Kaiju rule the earth.

Three years have passed since the US government attempted to use giant mechs to fight off an incursion of kaiju. The eight most powerful kaiju have carved up North America into their respective territories and their mutant offspring also roam the continent. The remnants of humanity are gathered in a remote settlement with Steel Samurai, the last of the remaining mechs, as their only protection. The mech is piloted by Captain Chris Myers who realizes that humanity will not survive if they stay at the settlement. In order to preserve the human race, he leaves the settlement unprotected as he engages on a desperate plan to draw the eight kaiju into each other's territories. His hope is that the kaiju will destroy each other. Chris will encounter horrors including the amorphous Amebos, Tortiraus the Giant turtle, and the nuclear powered mutant dinosaur Atomic Rex!

KAIJU DEADFALL
by JE Gurley

Death from space. The first meteor landed in the Pacific Ocean near San Francisco, causing an earthquake and a tsunami. The second wiped out a small Indiana city. The third struck the deserts of Nevada. When gigantic monsters Ishom, Girra, and Nusku emerge from the impact craters, the world faces a threat unlike any it had ever known - Kaiju. NASA catastrophist Gate Rutherford and Special Ops Captain Aiden Walker must find a way to stop the creatures before they destroy every major city in America..

SEVERED**PRESS**

facebook.com/severedpress
twitter.com/severedpress

CHECK OUT OTHER GREAT KAIJU NOVELS

POLAR YETI AND THE BEASTS OF PREHISTORY
by Matthew Dennion

A team from Princeton University searching for a lost tribe in Antartica discover a hidden valley filled with wooly mammoths, saber toothed tigers and other Ice Age beasts. Seizing the opportunity of a lifetime, the team set up camp to study the amazing creatures. But there is something else that lives in the Valley. Something terrifying. Something beyond imagination. POLAR YETI!

TITAN WARS
by M.C. Norris

Millions of microscopic alien life forms escape a sample canister of water from the frigid depths of outer space. Invisible to the naked eye, a menacing menagerie of more than seventy deadly species react to Earth's warm and fertile seas by launching into metabolic overdrive. Waves of gargantuan abominations begin to rise from the sea, transforming our world into a zoo without cages, where humans plunge to the bottom of the food chain.

In dire need of a zookeeper, the Allied Navy turns to "Psyjack," a bickering geek squad with an outrageous plan to hack into the minds of the megafauna with some reengineered neurosurgical technology. The young gamers hope to level the uneven playing field by fighting monsters with monsters, but they couldn't have anticipated how deadly their technology could be, if it ever fell into the wrong hands ...

Made in the USA
San Bernardino, CA
29 May 2020

72442195R00090